D0605939

A Treasury of

CHRISTMAS STORIES

A Treasury of CHRISTMAS STORIES

Webb Garrison

Rutledge Hill Press
Nashville, Tennessee

Published in Nashville, Tennessee, by Rutledge Hill Press,
513 Third Avenue South, Nashville, Tennessee 37210

Typography by Bailey Typography, Nashville, Tennessee

Library of Congress Cataloging-in-Publication Data

A treasury of Christmas stories / Webb Garrison.
p. cm.
Includes index.
ISBN 1-55853-087-8
1. Christmas stories, American. I. Garrison, Webb B.
PS648.C45T74 1990 90-41071
813.008'033—dc20 CIP

Printed in the United States of America
1 2 3 4 5 6 7 8 — 95 94 93 92 91 90

Contents

Contents continued

Men and Women at Their Creative Best

Of all the seasons, Christmas is my favorite. Not only are "creatures made in the image of God" at their best during this time, at Christmas we are reminded that the events we celebrate continue to affect our lives for good nearly two thousand years later.

As Christmas is unique among the seasons, I believe the volume you are reading is unique among books about Christmas. Certainly, many books have been written, most of them concentrating upon Christmas carols and celebrations, fruit cake and candlelight, doll houses and gingerbread castles, handmade ornaments and toys, or stories written to inspire children or adults.

A *Treasury of Christmas Stories* is deliberately different from them.

In this volume I have collected some of my favorite stories related to the Christmas season. All of them deal with real persons and historical events, although I am sure that in some instances oral tradition has filled in gaps for which historical documentation has not been available. I have used those traditions freely, and much of the dialogue represents what persons may reasonably be considered to have said given the circumstances.

These stories illustrate the soaring human spirit that finds new energy at this time of the year. Many significant events that have taken place during the Christmas season might never have occurred were it not that Christmas changes us, even if only for a moment sometimes.

Here are stories of people who have gone the extra mile to find creative ways to give, who have begun some of the traditions that we treasure most, and who have made unusual accomplishments during this season.

Have I exhausted the treasure of stories that could be told?

Not on your life!

This book is but an introduction to the off-trail lore of the season, an appetizer, not a seven-course holiday feast. As it entertains and inspires you, and perhaps informs you some, hopefully it will provide you with motivation to look more carefully into how the season of the coming of the Babe in a manger has affected the course of mankind.

—Webb Garrison

Lake Junaluska, North Carolina

A Treasury of CHRISTMAS STORIES

Part One

'Tis the Season to Be Giving

The joy of giving has inspired many unusual gifts. Some of these gifts were made by notables whose names are familiar to all. Others were conceived and given by people who were not well known in their time, many whose names are no longer remembered. Nevertheless, a gift is a gift, and during the season of Christmas sometimes love has been surpassed by creativity!

An Unusual Gift

"ARE YOU SORRY YOU CAME TO SAMOA?"

"Certainly not! Scotland is charming, but it is wet and cold much of the year. I'll always believe that's why I had so much lung trouble as a child."

"I find it hard to believe that you've ever had physical problems. You're always so cheerful."

Robert L. Stevenson

Robert Louis Stevenson, age forty-one, smiled as he looked around the room at his twelve guests. Invited to Stevenson's sprawling mansion, Vailima, they were enjoying the lively conversation.

"Do you often hurt, here at Vailima?" a guest asked.

"The people on this island call me Tusitala, their name for 'Teller of Tales.' If I told you I am seldom in pain, I would really be Tusitala tonight," Stevenson laughed.

"But let's talk about how we all came to this lovely place. I volunteer to break the ice, although I must admit it may be a bit hard to do in Samoa!"

When the laughter subsided, the author of *A Child's Garden of Verses, Dr. Jekyll and Mr. Hyde,* and *Kidnapped* continued. "There were no regular steamers calling here in those days, so we chartered a little boat. It pitched and rolled so badly that we were thoroughly miserable. I think I have never been so glad to get solid ground under my feet.

"But the delay brought about by taking that little boat changed our schedule. Although we had planned to arrive no later than November 30, we didn't get here until a few days before Christmas.

"We knew it was Christmas, not from the weather but from the calendar. That made us feel even farther from Scotland. Most of you had not arrived here yet. Talk about a lonely Christmas! If it had not

Stevenson's Vailima, about 1893

been for the friendly natives, we might have felt sorry for ourselves!"

"I was not here, but I can sympathize," Henry C. Ide, the newly arrived U.S. land commissioner, interjected.

"Christmas is the most difficult time of the year at our house. Our first child, Annie, was born on December 25. Almost as soon as she began to walk and talk, she let us know that she felt cheated. Now she's fourteen, and she has never had a proper birthday party."

"What a shame!" exclaimed Stevenson. "Birthday parties are part of growing up. Annie is right. She has been cheated, and we must do something about it."

The "Teller of Tales" got Annie's address from her father, and after his guests had departed, he drew upon his legal training to prepare, in his own handwriting, a deed of gift:

> I, Robert Louis Stevenson, advocate of the Scots Bar, author of *The Master of Ballantrae* and *Moral Emblems,* civil engineer, sole owner and patenter of the palace and plantation known as Vailima, in the island of Upohi, Samoa, a British subject, being in sound mind and pretty well, I thank you, in body;

In consideration that Miss Annie H. Ide, daughter of H. C. Ide, in the town of St. Johnsbury, in the County of Caledonia, in the State of Vermont, United States of America, was born, out of all reason, upon Christmas Day, and is therefore, out of all justice, denied the consolation and profit of a proper birthday;

And considering that I, the said Robert Louis Stevenson, having attained an age when, oh, we never mention it, and that I have no further use for a birthday of any description;

And in consideration that I have met H. C. Ide, the father of the said Annie H. Ide, and have found him about as white a Land Commissioner as I require;

Have transferred and do hereby transfer to the said Annie H. Ide, all and whole, my rights and privileges in the thirteenth day of November, formerly my birthday, now, hereby, and henceforth the birthday of the said Annie H. Ide, to have, hold, exercise, and enjoy the same in the customary manners, by the sporting of fine raiment, eating of rich meats and receipt of gifts, compliments, and copies of verse, according to the manner of our ancestors.

Robert L. Stevenson as sketched by his wife, Fanny Osborne

And I direct the said Annie H. Ide to add to her said name the name of Louisa—at least in private; and I charge her to use my said birthday with moderation and humanity, the said birthday not being so young as it once was, and having carried me in a very satisfactory manner since I can remember. In case the said Annie H. Ide shall neglect or contravene either of the above conditions, I hereby revoke the donation, and transfer my rights in the said birthday to the President of the United States of America, for the time being.

In witness whereof I have hereto set my hand and seal this nineteenth day of June in the year of Grace, eighteen hundred and ninety-one.

Robert Louis Stevenson

WITNESS: Lloyd Osbourne
WITNESS: Harold Watts

After it was signed, sealed, and witnessed, this handwritten document was dispatched to Vermont.

Late in November, Stevenson received from Annie "Louisa" a letter thanking him for his gift. "For the first time in my life, I have had a real birthday party," she told him. "You know the date, of course. It was November 13, 1891. Thank You!"

Stevenson's mother, who heard of the matter, wrote her son to tell him that since he had given away his birthday, he should no longer expect presents. "For old times' sake, however," she added, "I am willing to pay for a bathroom to be added to Vailima."

Stevenson wrote his mother a letter of thanks, but he warned her that Annie Louisa might have a legal claim to the new room.

Eighteen months later, by joint action of England, Germany, and the United States, Henry C. Ide was named chief justice of Samoa. During his tenure in this post, the daughter to whom Stevenson had given his birthday and who had taken Louisa as her name, visited Samoa and met her benefactor.

Robert Louis Stevenson survived the gift of his birthday for only three and one-half years. Death came to the Teller of Tales when he was barely forty-four, at the approach of the season that prompted him to draft his whimsical deed to the "Christmas child" of a new friend.

Stevenson and his family were surrounded by native servants.

Escape to Freedom

"YOU'D BETTER FIX UP BOTH PASSES. I CAN'T write very good."

"I thought I might have to do that. I have an old pass I can copy. How should I date them?"

"Mark mine for four days, beginning Thursday. Maybe you'd better let yours start a day earlier. Four days won't attract any attention, but I think we'd better have 'em start a day apart."

"That's right," Ellen Craft agreed. "The least little thing could give us away. You sure you'll have everything else ready?"

"Positive," replied her husband, William Craft. "But now that I think about it, two passes from your mistress might be noticed. Maybe I can talk old Simpson into fixing up one for me."

"Sure," Ellen replied thoughtfully. "I think he'll give it to you. But if he won't, let me know by nighttime so I can make one for you. I think I can write his name."

So William Craft returned to the carpentry shop where he worked to earn cash for his owner. He explained that he had never seen the ocean and had saved up enough money to buy a railroad ticket. Simpson, his part-time employer, grumbled but wrote out a four-day pass that would permit the slave to make the round trip between Macon and Savannah, Georgia.

Ellen Craft posed as a "gentleman from middle Georgia."

Craft had reached Macon, the largest city in central Georgia, some time during the early 1840s. As an adolescent, he had been apprenticed to a carpenter for a time, which made him more valuable than most slaves. Any slave who had mastered a trade could be hired out at a good rate.

Not long after reaching Macon, the youthful black carpenter became enamored with a new acquaintance, Ellen. Her first owner had been her father, a commonplace relationship in that time. Nearly white, she often was thought by strangers to be a granddaughter of her second owner, the elderly white woman to whom she was sold as a small girl.

When she was about eleven years old, Ellen was given to her second owner's daughter as a wedding present. Taken to Macon after the ceremony, she lived there in comfort.

William Craft, who later wrote an account of their escape.

Once she met William Craft, however, her life of tranquility vanished. They fell in love, but the law forbade them to marry. However, in a secret slave ceremony held in 1846, they became man and wife in the eyes of the black community.

Although strict laws prohibited owners from permitting anyone to teach their slaves to read and write, William and Ellen learned on their own. But William was less skilled at writing than Ellen was.

He did have good hearing, though, and he knew how to listen carefully. Somehow he managed to be standing nearby when a Fourth of July orator quoted the Declaration of Independence: "We hold these truths to be self-evident, that all men are created equal . . ."

What a thought! Equality!

William did not know that our nation's founding fathers had not intended their noble words to apply to blacks. He tried to imagine what it would be like to be equal to white men, and free.

Soon Ellen and William were obsessed with freedom. First they began to talk guardedly about escaping to freedom, but before long they were thinking in practical terms. Fashioning one scheme after another, they dreamed about how they might win their freedom. First they thought of fleeing to Canada, or maybe Boston, as itinerant peddlers. After they began discussing this idea, they soon saw how impractical it was.

As the Christmas season drew near, however, they found inspiration. Light-skinned Ellen would travel as a man, and William would be "his" black attendant.

* * *

Ellen did not have to prepare a forgery. Her mistress cheerfully gave her a commonplace Christmas gift: a pass that permitted her to go on a visit for a few days.

William had found a paying job as a waiter in a hotel and had hoarded his earnings. That made it possible for him to buy an entire outfit of clothing, except for trousers. Assembled piece by piece, the disguise was nearly complete when Ellen finished sewing a pair of rough homespun pants by hand.

With her head wrapped in a handkerchief to conceal her lack of beard, the slightly tan woman headed for Savannah for the holidays with her black slave in attendance. She attracted no attention.

Careful to avoid contact with each other, William and Ellen traveled in separate cars of the train. They reached the seaport in less than twenty-four hours after leaving Macon.

It was easy to book passage on a ship from Savannah to Charleston. From there they expected to go directly to Philadelphia, but they found that no vessel in the harbor was bound for the city.

Required to go by way of Wilmington, North Carolina, the "young gentleman from Georgia" was told to fill out a form listing his name and address. Fearful that her poor handwriting might give her away,

Savannah harbor about 1860, first major stop on the way to Philadelphia.

Philadelphia waterfront [ENGRAVING BY GEORGE HEAP AND NICHOLAS SCISS]

Ellen had prepared for such an emergency by wrapping her hands in salve-soaked rags, claiming severe rheumatism.

"Makes no difference at all," the ship's officer explained. "The law requires that the passenger list be filled out with names and addresses. Can't take you unless it's done."

Ellen turned to a young military officer with whom she had become acquainted on the trip from Savannah. Somewhat inebriated, he vouched for his new friend, then used the information she supplied to fill out the passenger list with a flourish.

Their ship docked in the eerie predawn light of winter. After inquiring for directions, William and Ellen Craft trudged toward the point at which they hoped to be met by Quakers who would take them in and hide them, in spite of the Fugitive Slave Law.

That is how two ragged refugees from the land of King Cotton came to be sitting on the steps of Independence Hall holding hands as the sun rose above the horizon on Christmas Day 1848.

"Free!" William exulted.

"Yes. It's Christmas Day. And we're really free!"

Charleston Custom House, whose agents checked rosters of ships.

A Gift from the President

"CHRISTMAS GIFT, MR. WELLES! CHRISTMAS gift!"

"You don't miss a trick, do you, Billy?" Gideon Welles chuckled. "I'll try to remember you before the holidays are over, but right now, I have a lot of things that the president needs to see."

"All those papers, Mr. Welles? And this nice young lady, too? I'll take you right up."

With those words manservant Billy Slade led the U.S. secretary of the navy and a plain looking young woman up a private stairway to the hallway outside the office of Abraham Lincoln. There he signaled the president's chief secretary.

"Here he is, Mr. Nicolay. Just like you said."

"Good morning, Mr. Welles. I see you have brought the usual bundle of applications for holiday clemency. And this year you have not come alone . . ."

"This is Miss Laura Jones. She'll wait for me while I am in the office. Miss Jones, this is Mr. John Nicolay, secretary to the president."

"Glad to meet you, Miss Jones," Nicolay was quick to reply. "Just take a seat against the wall. I'll get you inside as soon as I can."

Turning to Gideon Welles, he continued. "Mr. Welles, have you cleared with Mr. Stanton this year?"

"Of course not. The secretary of war does not see eye to eye with me on the matter of clemency. And until Mr. Lincoln says otherwise, I am in charge of the U.S. Navy.

"I have been here every Christmas, and so far Mr. Lincoln and I have not had a violent disagreement over so much as one case."

U.S. Secretary of the Navy Gideon Welles

"Certainly, sir," Nicolay answered. "I meant no disrespect. But it is common talk in the capital that you present more cases than any other member of the cabinet and that Mr. Stanton wishes you were less lenient and persistent."

"Stanton has only the army to think about. I am charged with guarding 3,500 miles of coastline with blockade runners operating along nearly every mile. Some of them are just innocent fishermen who are trying to make a living and have been tricked into smuggling goods for the Confederacy.

"Besides, I don't have the final word. Mr. Lincoln makes the decisions, and Stanton and I both are subordinates. I do nothing more than plead cases that would otherwise be overlooked."

"Well, you have a reputation for eloquence in pleading, sir," Nicolay responded. "I believe Mr. Lincoln is expecting you. Go right in. I'll wait here with Miss Jones."

Seated across the desk from President Lincoln, Gideon Welles wasted no time.

"You are very busy, sir. I will try to move quickly since there are more requests this year than usual."

When Lincoln took office, the unfinished capitol was visible from the White House.

"Why are there more?"

"Because our people—and the Rebels, too—are weary of war. They're taking more foolish chances, and they're getting themselves into more trouble. Here. I'll just hand the petitions to you, one by one, as usual. If you have any questions, I'll do the best I can with them."

Halfway through the thick sheaf of petitions, Welles was startled by Tad Lincoln, the president's youngest son, who jumped on him from behind.

"Let me guess," Welles laughed. "It must be one of Santa's elves!"

"No! No! Tad!" the boy cried. "Giddap, horsy," he shouted, tugging at the long beard of the secretary of the navy.

Accustomed to having the run of the White House, the boy often crept into his father's office on all fours to surprise a distinguished visitor. Welles, who had encountered Tad many times, twisted his head so he could look him in the eye.

Tad Lincoln grew calm when his father read to him [NATIONAL ARCHIVES].

"I hope you've been a good boy this year so old Santa can be good to you."

"Yep!"

"I hear that your father often reads to your brother and you at Christmas. Tomorrow is the big day. Are you going to eat turkey?"

"No turk! No!" the boy shouted. Sliding from his perch, he ran from the room crying.

"Now what on earth did I do to start the waterworks, Mr. President?"

"You couldn't have known it," Lincoln laughed, "but you said the wrong thing. Tad has a pet turkey, and he positively refuses to listen to talk of eating it.

"I've jotted down my decisions on the bottoms of the pages. Both of us are likely to be criticized for being too easy on men who have committed wrongs against this Union. But, now that I've laid myself open to new accusations from my opponents, what else does Mr. Secretary have up his sleeve?"

"Just one thing, sir. I have a request. Here it is . . ."

"Who is this Laura Jones?"

"A young woman from Virginia, sir. She has been working at Willard's Hotel, where my wife became acquainted with her some time ago."

"This Laura Jones is a Rebel female, I take it."

"Yes, sir. She tells my wife that her loyalty is to Virginia. Now she wants to go to Richmond to be married."

The streets of Washington swarmed with soldiers, bitter at not getting Christmas leaves.

"You know quite well that regulations forbid such a trip through our lines. I have commuted a good many sentences at your request, but I think the president of the United States does not have the authority to honor the request of this Laura Jones."

"Maybe not, sir. But you're also the commander-in-chief of the United States Navy, and the army as well."

Abraham Lincoln nodded soberly. "Responsibilities that I often wish I did not have."

"But they also give you opportunities, sir. As commander-in-chief, you can, if you wish, issue a military order permitting this young woman to go to her sweetheart. It would be a splendid Christmas gift to her, sir."

"If she wished to go to Wilmington or Savannah, it would be a fairly simple matter," Lincoln replied. "But Richmond is the capital of the Confederacy. She's practically asking me to commit an act of treason."

"Not quite that, sir. And Laura Jones is waiting in the hallway, hoping that you will talk to her yourself. May I bring her in?"

"I suppose so, but only for a moment. I still have a great deal of business to conduct, and it is Christmas Eve."

After the president talked briefly with Laura Jones, he abruptly returned to his office where he wrote out and signed an order that permitted her to pass through military lines to Richmond. The young woman would be married during the holidays.

Gideon Welles noted the incident in his diary. Also, to his chief clerk, William Faxon, he is said to have confided: "We got the pass. The president has always liked to select special things—not always costly, but rich in meaning—for those close to him. He didn't say so today, but I believe he knows in his heart that this pass for a Confederate girl is Abraham Lincoln's most splendid Christmas gift, ever."

A Santa for the Money Handlers

"WE SEEM TO HAVE CONCLUDED ALL OUR regular quarterly business. I will pronounce the meeting adjourned, unless someone has new business to propose."

"I'd like to call attention to the fact that today is exactly six months before Christmas Day."

"Of course, Mr. Hersey. It's June twenty-fifth. What is remarkable about that?"

"In my years here at Howard Banking, I don't recall that we've ever met on June twenty-fifth," head teller George E. Hersey responded.

"Matter of fact, you're right," interjected a member of the board of directors. "My father put me here soon after I started to shave, and I have missed very few meetings. None has ever been held six months to the day before Christmas. What do you make of this, George?"

"The date has set me to thinking that maybe we could do something to put a little Christmas joy into the hearts of bankers."

"Like what, for instance?"

"Well, maybe issue a special piece of currency. We could put something special on it. Just enough to make everybody who handles it take notice and spend a minute or two counting his blessings."

"How about a three-dollar bill? I hear some of them are floating around in the South. That would make a fellow stop and think!"

President Charles Ellis objected. "Currency of odd denominations is plentiful, but Mr. Howard is right. It would be nice to emphasize Christmas ahead of the season. Along about Thanksgiving every year, people begin to pull out their ragged old Continental currency and bring it to us, hoping it will be worth something.

"Paper issued by the Continental Congress comes in all sizes, and it would be practically impossible to come up with a denomination that hasn't been used. The Continental Congress put out paper worth anywhere from six Spanish dollars to that ridiculous sixty-five-dollar bill that is beginning to become a collector's item.

"If we decide to follow Mr. Hersey's suggestion, I think we ought to concentrate on the art, not the size or shape or denomination."

"I strongly agree," Hersey said. "I've taken a look at some of the stuff that comes to us here in Boston. We don't get a lot from the South, but engravings of cotton show up on the issues of several states."

"There's no need to try to find a fresh face from the Revolution," Ellis said. "With every state printing its own currency for the last thirty years, all of the famous Americans were used long ago. What about a nice fireside scene, maybe with 'Merry Christmas' engraved below it?"

"That would be better than nothing," Hersey agreed, "but before I introduced the subject of Christmas money, I gave considerable attention to what we might put on it. As far as I know, no state or bank or mercantile house has issued currency carrying a picture of Santa Claus.

"I know the average citizen doesn't pay much attention to this European fellow. But most Germans do, and we have lots of them in Boston."

"It's not just Germans who are beginning to let their children hang stockings for Santa to fill on Christmas Eve. I like the idea. But what should he look like?" Ellis asked.

"Oh, he ought to be in a sleigh pulled by reindeer," Hersey replied, "maybe wearing a cocked hat. The back of the sleigh could be filled with presents. And Santa Claus should have a stub of a beard, I think."

"Your suggestion obviously is not spontaneous," the bank president commented. "Since you have given so much thought to it, I, for one, am willing to vote for you to proceed with your idea. How long will it take to get something ready?"

Currency issued by the Continental Congress was still widely available in the 1850s.

"Six or eight months in Boston. Nobody here is equipped to do a quick job. But I have heard a lot about the New York firm of Rawdon, Wright, Hatch, and Edson."

"Sounds as though there are enough partners to spread the work around. Do you have any estimate of the time they will require to produce a new issue?" a director inquired.

"I've heard they can finish a rush job in as little as ninety days. If we tell them exactly what we want and issue an order, I believe we can have Santa Claus currency ready by the middle of October, maybe earlier."

"Good!" President Ellis responded. "Let's spread a little Christmas joy among bankers and merchants!

"I can use some of it myself. Put Santa Claus into the hands of as many persons as possible. Maybe on a ten?"

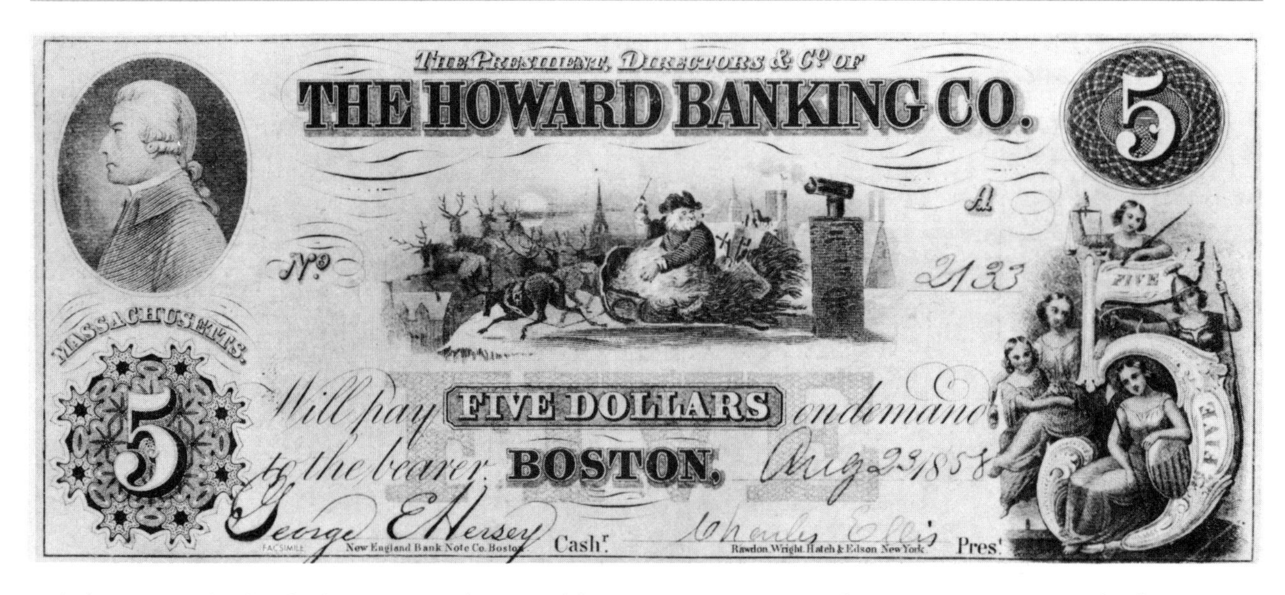

Only known U.S. legal tender bearing the image of Santa Claus.

"That would attract attention, of course," Hersey replied. "But we have to remember that twice as many fives circulate as tens."

"A factor to be taken into consideration, gentlemen," Ellis agreed. "Will those of you who favor issuing a ten-dollar Santa Claus bill for use this fall and thereafter please raise your hands? Now those who lean toward putting Saint Nick on a five?

"The fives have it. Mr. Hersey, we are indebted to you for your idea, and we authorize you to pursue it immediately."

In late September 1858 a Santa Claus appeared whose looks followed traditions familiar to Dutch traders who were New York's first European settlers. Like most currency of the era, the Santa Claus five was printed in black ink. "Greenbacks," issued by the federal government, would not make their appearance until a time of fiscal crisis during the Civil War.

Circulated almost entirely in and around Boston, the special Christmas currency is now a rare collector's item. It depicts a heavy-loaded, reindeer-drawn sleigh flying from the chimney of a snow-topped roof while a pipe-smoking Santa gazes backward, almost as though he wants to be sure he left the right goodies at his last stop.

The Spirit of Giving Invaded Savannah

"IS IT TRUE ABOUT THE GENERAL'S GIFT?"

"What gift?"

"His Christmas gift to Old Abe."

"Don't know what you're talking about, private."

Digging into his pocket, a ragged member of the 33rd Indiana Militia pulled out a scrap of paper and handed it to his lieutenant. "Here. Read it. They say it's a copy of a telegram that went out this morning."

Squinting, the officer peered at the scribbled message, pondered it silently, then read it aloud:

General William T. Sherman's "Christmas gift to Lincoln" set off a chain reaction.

Savannah, Georgia
December 22, 1864

To His Excellency President Lincoln,
Washington, D.C.:

I beg to present to you as a Christmas-gift the city of Savannah, with one hundred and fifty heavy guns and plenty of ammunition, also about twenty-five thousand bales of cotton.

W. T. Sherman
Major-General

"How many men know about this, private?"

"Don't know, but a lot. Copies are just about everywhere. Is it sure enough real?"

"Of course. No one else but the general would address the president as 'Excellency.' And the figures for heavy guns and bales of cotton are just about right. I saw a report from the Quartermaster Corps last night.

"Seems a sorta strange Christmas gift. No one but General Sherman would think of such a thing.

"But we are at our destination, and it is not much more than forty-eight hours until Christmas. That telegram has given me an idea. Let's give some of the hungry Rebels a big dinner as a Christmas gift."

"Do you mean it, sir?"

Upon reaching Savannah, Sherman's troops were greeted by Union sailors.

"Of course I mean it. Hurry up to the 58th and the 100th and tell 'em to come help us. If their colonels ask why, just say that the spirit of giving has hit Savannah like a bombshell."

News of the plan to provide a feast for civilians was greeted with groans when word reached tents of the 4th Minnesota Veteran Volunteer Infantry.

"We've been starving ourselves for two weeks," a corporal protested. "There's plenty of good food here in Savannah, but back near Ebenezer Creek I watched a mule skinner drive his animal into a swamp until it was hip-deep in water. When the mule couldn't run or balk, he shot him between the eyes, then took the meat to the mess tent. Believe me, that 'prime steak' didn't last long!"

"We had plenty to eat until we came near the coast. What happened then?"

"I think the difference is in the land. No fine plantations around here, at least not many. Back in central Georgia, you saw a plantation everywhere you looked."

"Sure, I remember. But lately some of us have been as hungry as a pack of bitch wolves caught in a snowdrift. I saw one fellow scratching in pine straw, looking for corn left by the horses."

"That must have been last week. Horses ain't had no corn lately. They're mean and wild from eatin' nothing but rice straw."

"Now that we're straddling Savannah, everything is different. Cook says he's got all the fixings for the best Christmas dinner you ever ate. It might not be such a bad idea to divide a little of it with the Rebs."

Spreading through the huge Federal encampment by word of mouth, the "great idea" of an unidentified Indiana lieutenant met with some objections. But so many veterans of the "march to the sea" thought it was such a splendid idea that it mushroomed as it spread.

Leading citizens and their ladies were required to get passes — here distributed by General Geary — in order to move about the countryside.

On Christmas Eve a hand-picked contingent of about one hundred officers and men loaded a wagon caravan whose destination was a region picked clean of food by Union and Confederate forces. The wagons contained bushels of baked sweet potatoes and roasted chickens and turkeys. One wagon was piled high with pork; another carried only oysters: roasted, fried, and raw for eating on the half shell.

At their destination, the blue-clad soldiers found a ragged band of civilians. Blacks and whites alike gathered for the feast.

"We even brought salt and pepper!" one of the drivers yelled.

"Wait a minute!" an officer directed. "Don't start unloading yet. We need a proper setting for a Christmas feast. Go cut some limbs off that big sycamore."

Soon the soldiers returned with bundles of branches, bare of leaves, and fastened them to the heads of mules to convert them into reindeer. As soon as everything was ready, the hungry watchers were told, "Pitch in and clean up everything!"

For years, participants in one of the most unusual of all Christmas dinners told their relatives and friends about it. One of them observed, "For two blessed hours that day, there were no Northerners and no Southerners, no Federals and no Confederates—just a happy band of people joined in the bond of giving and receiving."

Until near the coast, Federal "bummers" seized foodstuffs and animals, then hunted valuables of civilians.

The happy soldiers, some of whom had wiped their eyes as they watched the feast, returned to the camps with another idea. "Break out the sweetest hay that you can find," they directed, "and give it to the horses. They deserve something special today, too."

In beleaguered Savannah, whose twenty thousand civilian inhabitants had not experienced starvation, Pennsylvania-born General John W. Geary knew that no one was hungry. Nevertheless, caught up in the excitement of making Christmas memorable, he strode into his headquarters kitchen without announcement. Startled, black cooks and dishwashers and aides tried awkwardly to come to attention.

"At ease, ladies and gentlemen," Geary ordered. "I simply want to know which of you are free and which are slaves."

To his surprise, only one worker—a young woman—raised her hand to signify that she still considered herself a slave, even though she was now far from her master. Geary questioned her and discovered that a tall cook named Samuel had taken her as his wife in a secret slave ceremony back on a nearby plantation.

"Come, Samuel," the general directed, "and stand beside me."

He then turned to the young woman, placed her hand in Samuel's, and said, "Samuel, I take great pleasure in presenting you with a Christmas gift, your wife, Sally, who is now a free woman!"

Meanwhile, from the nation's capital, Abraham Lincoln sent General Sherman a long telegram of thanks for his Christmas gift. And in and around the one-time Confederate city, many civilians vowed to remember that Yankees could sometimes be kind and generous.

The President's Gift List

TWENTY-SEVEN-YEAR-OLD GENTLEMAN FARMER George Washington found himself facing something new in 1759. For the first time, he had to select Christmas gifts for children.

Until he began courting a lovely young widow, Washington had had few contacts with small boys or girls. At age fifteen he was working as a surveyor, and later he served in the British army during the French and Indian War. Although he won rapid promotion, in 1758 Colonel Washington resigned his commission and retired to his brother's estate.

It had been known as Little Hunting Plantation, but the name of the five-thousand-acre estate was changed when George's half-brother Lawrence bought it in 1743. As a token of respect for Admiral Edward Vernon of the British Navy, the place was renamed Mount Vernon. It was to this estate that George Washington retired from the military to become a farmer.

Artist's interpretation of George Washington's first visit with Martha Custis.

Soon after beginning his life as a farmer, Washington began calling upon a neighbor, Mrs. Martha Dandridge Custis, a widow who had inherited 17,000 acres of land and 150 slaves from her husband. She was considered the wealthiest eligible woman in all Virginia.

"I expected to concentrate upon raising tobacco," he explained to her during an early visit. "It did not take me long to discover my folly. Under the law, I found myself required to send the entire crop to Britain to be sold, carried there at my expense in British ships. Since I have no control over tobacco, I hope to diversify and produce things that can be sold here in America."

Made bold by the widow's encouragement of his agricultural plans, Washington asked for Martha Custis's hand in marriage. She agreed to marry him, and January 6, 1759, was selected as their wedding day. It would be a "grand affair" at Martha's home, the White House.

The bride wore a fashionable gown for the ceremony, and the groom was splendid in a silver-and-blue suit trimmed in red and adorned with gold knee buckles. Both five-year-old Jacky (John Parke) and three-year-old Patsy (Martha Parke), children of the bride, took part in the festivities.

Mrs. Martha Dandridge Custis Washington [WASHINGTON AND LEE UNIVERSITY]

Within weeks after the newlyweds and their children had taken up residence at Mount Vernon, George Washington began thinking about Christmas. It was still months away, but he would have to arrange for specialty items to be sent from far away Britain.

Some time during late spring, he dispatched a list to one of his purchasing agents, the English firm of Robert Cary and Company. As Christmas presents for Jacky and Patsy, he prepared a handwritten list of orders for "miniatures":

A bird on Bellows
A Cuckoo
A turnabout Parrot
A Grocers Shop
An Aviary
A Prussian Dragoon
A man Smoakg
A Tunbridge Tea Sett
3 Neat Tunbridge Toys
A Neat Book Fash Tea Chest
A box best Household Stuff
A straw Patch box w. a Glass
A neat dress'd Was Baby

Did George Washington consult the children's mother, his bride? Or did he carefully select the toys and gifts without help? Nothing in his voluminous papers and records gives even a hint.

Washington's spelling and punctuation were inconsistent, leaving much to be desired by modern standards. Some scholars have inter-

Mount Vernon at Christmas Eve, 1798

preted one perplexing line as listing two items. Thus, with punctuation added, he requested "A neat book; fash. tea chest."

Any parent knows that a girl of three would be glad to have a fashionable tea chest and a neat book! Such a tea chest would go admirably with the "Tunbridge tea sett."

Tunbridge (or Tonbridge) ware was manufactured and sold in a market town about thirty miles southeast of London. The name of the town was bestowed upon goods that could be secured only there. Much Tunbridge ware was made of wood, carefully ornamented with inlaid holly, a wood noted for its even substance and hardness.

Characteristically, young Washington did not simply order a tea set for his stepdaughter. He specified that she must have a Tunbridge tea set and nothing less.

Washington's diary entries for a few years, including 1759 and

1760, are missing. Only fragments of miscellaneous papers, including the order that took six weeks to reach England, have been preserved. So there is no way to know if Jacky and Patsy got all of their gifts on December 25, 1759. Long delays in shipment were commonplace in that era. But there can be no doubt that Washington took more than ordinary care to try to get a special set of Christmas gifts for his stepchildren.

At age twenty-six, Washington took off his uniform, expecting never again to put one on.

Their needs and wants were reflected in other purchase orders placed with Robert Cary and Company.

In September 1759, Washington ordered clothing for both children, plus "6 little books for Childn. begg. to Read" and "10 shillings worth of Toys."

A few months earlier, newly married Washington received from Unwin and Company of London a shipment that included, according to his personal records:

A childs Fiddle
A Coach and 6 in a box
A corn'r Cupboard
A filigree Watch and chains
A stable w' 6 horses
A Neat Walnut Bureau
A Toy Whip
A Neat Enamld Watch box

Regardless of earlier and later purchase orders sent to England on behalf of "Master Jacky" and "Mistress Patsy," the list of 1759 speaks volumes. More than formal documents could, it reveals that the Father of His Country was busy very early in the year, trying to make Christmas special for the two children he had gained by marriage.

A Belated Christmas Gift

"ANOTHER BELATED GIFT, SIR, BROUGHT BY A messenger."

"Take care of it, please, James."

"I would if I could, but the fellow insists that he is required to hand it to you personally."

"Show him in, then. But be sure to tell him I am very busy and he must not waste words."

James Ingraham stepped back to the door of the mansion and returned with a mud-spattered courier. "Mr. Flagler will see you, there at his desk. But you must be brief."

"Why couldn't you hand that package to Mr. Ingraham, at the door?"

"Because Mrs. Tuttle would skin me alive if I took her money and didn't do as she said."

"Mrs. Julia Tuttle of Biscayne Bay?"

"Yes, sir. She told me to tell you that she has sent a very special Christmas present. I'm sorry it is so late. I left at sunup on the twenty-fifth, but it's a long way from her place to St. Augustine."

"Mr. Ingraham knows. He was there a year or so ago. He will show you out. Here's a little 'thank you' for making the trip."

Henry Morrison Flagler took the package and hefted it. "Big," he commented as his aide returned, "but mighty light. Wonder what she's up to now. Open it, James, and take a look."

With only part of the wrapping paper removed, Ingraham caught a glimpse of the package's contents. "You won't believe it, sir!" he exclaimed. "Orange blossoms!"

"It must be one of Mrs. Tuttle's little pranks."

"No, sir. Real orange blossoms. Fresh, too."

Henry M. Flagler, friend and one-time partner of John D. Rockefeller [HENRY MORRISON FLAGLER MUSEUM]

"You don't suppose the woman has built herself a greenhouse, do you?"

"I wouldn't put anything past her," Ingraham laughed, "but these look like they came from outdoors. Here's a little note. Maybe it will explain."

"Read it to me, please. Then put the blossoms in a vase and get back to what you were doing when you were interrupted."

"Yes, sir. The note says:

> In a vast tract stretching from the Everglades to the Atlantic, orange blossoms escaped damage from the great freeze of Christmas Eve. Come and see for yourself. And enjoy a belated Merry Christmas!
>
> Always your sincere friend,
> Julia Tuttle

"Hand me the blossoms, James, and let me take a closer look. You don't suppose I've had you out spending a hundred thousand dollars needlessly, do you?"

"No, sir. Every penny you're putting into seeds and fertilizer is being well spent. Lots of farmers who were ready to pack up and go back north will get your help and decide to give oranges another try. I've already had maybe fifty commitments to stay, along with thanks for your generosity."

"Little enough. Really an investment in the future of Florida. There's no need to build hotels and railroads unless there are people here. Florida's future is tied to oranges. You've heard me say that often enough, haven't you?"

"Certainly, Mr. Flagler, and I think you did the right thing when you began handing out free seedlings to get people started. Nobody—not even the old crackers here—believed that the temperature would drop to eighteen degrees and wipe out the entire crop."

"All but the crop in and around Biscayne Bay," mused the multimillionaire who had decided that Florida was the best place to invest the fortune gained from his involvement in the Standard Oil Company. As his chief aide waited expectantly, Flagler pondered briefly, then broke the silence.

"I'll have to accept that invitation to visit. Right away. But how in the world will we manage to get to such a godforsaken place from here?"

"It won't be easy," James Ingraham admitted, "but it can be done. We can use the launch on New River, probably as far as Fort Lauderdale. Then we'll have to buy mules and a wagon for the rest of the trip."

"How long will it take?"

"Maybe three days. If we are lucky."

"No more than that? It could be worse. Make all the arrangements, and we will start the day after tomorrow."

Mrs. Julia Tuttle, "mother of Miami, Florida" [FLORIDA STATE ARCHIVES]

At her Biscayne Bay home, a remodeled military barracks that once belonged to abandoned Fort Dallas, Mrs. Julia Tuttle remembered the past as she waited hopefully for word from St. Augustine. Born and reared in Cleveland, Ohio, she first heard of Florida from her mother. Frances Sturtevant was proud of having taught in an Indian school at Tallahassee before her marriage. When the health of her husband, Ephraim, began to fail, the two of them went to the peninsula hoping that sunshine would restore his strength.

Their only child, Julia, had married Frederick Tuttle, an industrialist who dealt in large quantities of iron ore. Julia worked as a volunteer at Euclid Baptist Church in Cleveland, where her husband's family had long-standing ties with John D. Rockefeller.

"Your father gave me my first job when I was a struggling youngster," Rockefeller told Frederick many times. "I can never repay him for his kindness. So call upon me if I can be of help to you and your family."

Following Frederick's premature death from tuberculosis, Julia remembered the Rockefeller promise and decided to act upon it. "There are too many memories for me here in Cleveland," she told Rockefeller, who now headed the Standard Oil Company. "I have many pleasant associations with Florida through my mother. Someone told me that one of your associates, a Mr. Flagler, is living there and is in need of a housekeeper for his new hotel. I am thirty-seven years old and in good health. If you will give me a strong recommendation, I am sure I can get the job."

Rockefeller spoke with Flagler by telephone, then informed the young widow, "He will not give any personal attention to the running of his hotel when it is completed. And he is of the opinion that his manager, a Mr. Seavey, has already arranged in respect to the position you refer to."

Disappointed, but still keenly interested in Florida, Julia Tuttle visited the region in search of a suitable place to live. In the sleepy little fishing village of Miami, which she and her husband had visited earlier, she arranged to buy a 644-acre tract on the north side of the Miami River. Since the property included the two stone buildings of old Fort Dallas, she transformed one of them into a two-story residence. A kitchen, workshop, windmill, boathouse, and stable were added. About 150 acres were fenced for farming.

At intervals she contacted Henry Flagler, telling him about the area in which she lived and trying to persuade him to build a railroad to it. Always, he politely but firmly rejected her overtures.

Having attempted to make good use of the great freeze of 1894, she was sure that this time Flagler would come. Eagerly awaiting his arrival, Mrs. Tuttle put her son Harry to work.

"Cut the tallest sapling you can find," she instructed. "Lop off all the branches and make a flagpole, and put it as close to the house as you can. I have a flag that once belonged to your grandfather. When it flies from the top of the pole, our visitors will be able to see it from a considerable distance."

Accompanied by James Ingraham and two other aides, Henry M. Flagler knew the meaning of the flag as soon as he spotted it. "She's ready for us," he commented. "But I'm not sure we're ready for her."

Usually dapper, the man whose splendid railroad now extended to Palm Beach was bedraggled and travel weary. The mustache he usually tended with great care was tousled, and black swamp water had soiled his clothing from head to foot. Yet he was openly exuberant upon reaching his destination.

The Miami railroad station, about six years after Flagler picked its site [FLORIDA STATE ARCHIVES]

"Mrs. Tuttle," he exclaimed, "your special Christmas gift has brought me here, and as I look about I find it hard to believe that I am not, indeed, on the shores of paradise!"

"Then you will extend the railroad here?"

"Positively. I will have to build at least eighty miles of track, and that will take time. And we'll have to dredge a channel from the ocean to your front door. Otherwise, there's no way to make Miami a deep-sea port."

"Are you sure you will proceed?"

James Ingraham chuckled aloud. "You have had several contacts with Mr. Flagler, but you do not know him well," he pointed out. "Once he has made up his mind, he sticks with his decisions. Sometimes he moves slowly, but this time he is ready to go into action at once."

Within a few days, the industrialist selected sites for a railroad terminal and a splendid new hotel. "We'll put up at least three hundred rooms, maybe more," he told Ingraham. "Call it the Royal Palm, and be sure it is finished in lemon yellow. It must be ready for occupancy when the railroad arrives."

Once his railroad reached Biscayne Bay, Flagler decided to extend it to Key West to give Florida a rail line that extended from the northern border to the southern tip. Moving his residence from St. Augustine to Palm Beach, he erected Whitehall mansion, now open to visitors and complete with the private railroad car in which he customarily traveled.

Julia Tuttle did not live to see the long-range plans of Henry M. Flagler brought to fruition, and many of the people who have come to Florida from other regions have never heard of her. But true old-timers of the area have made her story into oral history. Consequently, the Ohio woman who sent orange blossoms at Christmas is remembered as the "mother of Miami."

The Rambler, *private railroad car of Flagler, now at Whitehall mansion.*

Part Two
The Many Faces of Santa Claus

Today every boy and girl is familiar with the appearance of Santa Claus. Whether he appears at a shopping mall in Madison, Wisconsin, or a department store in Los Angeles, he is chubby and bearded and is wearing a bright red suit.

It has not always been that way. Until recently, the "spirit of Christmas" was depicted in a variety of ways. And always, the artists were the only ones who claimed to have seen him in person.

The Beloved Saint Nicholas

HIS FACE PUFFED AND RED FROM WEEPING, SIMeon the silversmith bowed to acknowledge the presence of his oldest daughter. Eyes downcast, she waited for him to speak. After many minutes, he began haltingly, "Dearest Naomi, I do not need to tell you. We have eaten the last crumb of bread."

"Yes, Father. And my sisters and I have cut our sandals into narrow strips, soaked them overnight, and then chewed them. You do not need to tell me. I know what you must do."

"Then we will put on our best robes and go to the bazaar at noon the day after tomorrow. A wealthy merchant is expected there. If the bidding is spirited, you will fetch a fancy sum."

"Enough to save my sisters from being sold into a life of shame?"

"I wish I could make such a promise, dear Naomi, but, alas, I cannot. Unless the price of silver is cut in half, they, too, will have to go in time."

"I am resigned to my fate, Father. But Dorcas is not. When she learns that you have been forced to act, I fear for her."

"Dorcas is very young. You cannot expect a girl of fourteen to understand. No doubt she will spend the night on her knees, and Sarai is likely to join her."

"So will I, dear Father. But I understand. All five of us face starvation unless you act at once."

That night a lamp burned long past the usual hour in the home of the silversmith. But no one was afoot on the narrow streets of Patara in Asia Minor. Because robbers had been at work, a curfew imposed three years earlier, in A.D. 316, was still in effect.

As her father and sister had anticipated, Dorcas had dropped to her knees as soon as she learned what was to be done. "I shall keep a lamp burning and remain in prayer all night," she announced.

An hour before sunrise, the tired youngster began to doze while on her knees. Waking with a start, she faintly remembered having heard a strange noise. Or had she dreamed of it?

Looking about the room, she immediately noticed a leather pouch at the foot of the bed in which Naomi was sleeping near the chimney. Rubbing her eyes, Dorcas crawled across the floor to the pouch, pulled its leather strings apart, and found herself staring at a handful of gold coins.

"Father! Naomi! Mother! Sarai!" she screamed. "Look! God himself has answered my prayer!"

Crossing himself and mumbling a prayer, Simeon examined the coins carefully, then tested two of them with his teeth. "They really are gold!" he exulted. "We will not go to the bazaar after all, my daughter!"

Another pouch of gold appeared the following night. Clearly, it was meant to rescue the second virgin, Sarai, from a life of shame. On the third night young Dorcas put out the lamp at the usual hour, then sat, tense with hope and expectation, during hour after hour of darkness. Toward morning, she heard a dull thud as a third pouch of coins fell through the chimney. Racing to the door, she managed to catch a faint glimpse of a departing figure.

"Father! Father! Sisters! Mother!" she called. "Come quickly! Our own bishop, Nicholas himself, brought the gold!"

That is one of many versions of the story of "Saint Nicholas and the Three Virgins." Soon familiar throughout the Near East, the tale added to the fast-growing reputation of a man about whom few details are known. Believed to have been born in Patara in the province of Lycia, Nicholas entered the monastery of Sion some time late in the third century. In time he became an abbot, then was made bishop of Myra.

Nicholas of Myra, earliest embodiment of the spirit of Christmas, was the patron saint of children.

Many years before saving the daughters of Simeon the silversmith, Nicholas was on a voyage to the Holy Land when fierce winds threatened to overturn the small vessel in which he was sailing. In the face of this threat, the three seamen aboard dropped to their knees in fervent prayer. Nicholas made the sign of the cross, lifted his face to heaven, and prayed for calm weather. Miraculously, the wind ceased just as he said, "Amen." Naturally, his fellow passengers told everyone they met about the miracle.

Not long afterward, a wealthy traveler stopped in Myra for the night. Since no room in the inn was big enough to accommodate his retinue, his three sons were assigned a small but comfortable tent pitched next to the structure.

❧ Saint Nicholas became — next to Jesus Christ — the most revered figure in all Christendom.

Next morning, the three boys were missing. A search of the town yielded no clues, and their distraught father seemed on the verge of losing his mind. Nicholas heard of the tragedy, paid a personal visit to the father of the missing boys, and searched the neighborhood. In a salting tub only a few yards from the inn, he found three small bodies, clearly the victims of the innkeeper.

Nicholas prayed fervently, and in answer to his prayer the youngsters were restored to life. Their grateful father swore that he would take them on a pilgrimage to Jerusalem annually, as long as he lived.

Small wonder, then, that Nicholas's fame spread far and wide before his death on December 6, probably in A.D. 345. Soon he was widely revered as a saint, and it became customary to commemorate his gifts to the daughters of Simeon by giving gifts on the day of his death. Eventually, the date of this observance shifted to December 25.

Long before this change took place, Saint Nicholas had become—next to Jesus Christ—the most revered figure in all Christendom. He became the patron saint of Russia and of Greece, as well as of numerous European cities and of all sailors. No apostle of Jesus had so many churches dedicated to his memory as Saint Nicholas did, and he became identified with the spirit of giving at the season in which Christ was born.

Honored in many lands, the "boy bishop of Myra" was given a

Germany's Belsnickel was a fearful figure to children who were told they were bad.

variety of names. In each country he was depicted as wearing costumes from the area and riding animals native to the region.

In the Netherlands the name Saint Nicholas became Sinta Nikolaas and then Sinterklaas and Sancte Klaas. The Pennsylvania Dutch (Germans) transformed their homeland's Knecht Rupprecht into Belsnickel. He sometimes rode in a horse-drawn cart, but in Finland he often traveled astride a goat. Those lucky enough to catch a glimpse of him noted that his clothing varied from a short, brown smock to a green robe trimmed with gold. In Finland he wore a white-peaked cap accented in blue, but in the mountains of Bavaria he was seldom depicted without a bearskin cap.

Saint Nicholas was not always alone, but his assistant varied from region to region. In Switzerland his wife, Lucy, often accompanied him on his gift-giving rounds, while in Germany a grim-faced little monk followed him around with a sack into which he stuffed bad children. Black Piet, a Moor dressed as a medieval page, assisted Saint Nicholas in Holland.

In Finland the saint who personified the spirit of giving wore a long, white mustache; but in many sections of Europe his jet black beard made him look almost like a buccaneer. Usually depicted as tall and thin, he did not gain a paunch until modern times.

Literally a "man of a thousand faces," by the time of the Protestant Reformation Saint Nicholas was no longer seen as a boy bishop from Asia Minor. Instead, he took on whatever appearance people in various nations saw as appropriate for the one who brought goodies to children and switches or ashes to bad children.

Santa Made a Comeback

"CALL THE PEOPLE TOGETHER AND BRING THE flag," directed John Endicott of the Massachusetts Bay Colony. Assistant governor and one-sixth owner of the territory around Salem, he was known—and feared—for his religious zeal. Any man whose hair was too long was sure to be rebuked by him, while women who refused to wear long veils in public were subjected to harassment. With Governor John Winthrop temporarily absent, for the time being Endicott was the dominant figure in the struggling little colony.

Once his followers had assembled, Endicott selected an aide to hold the flag by a short staff. Whipping out a saber, the assistant governor attacked the flag from behind, ripping from it the red cross of Saint George.

That 1634 act of defiance was based on Endicott's long-standing hatred of anything he considered to smack of popery. In some respects it represented the high-water mark of Puritan revolt against tradition.

Pilgrims, as stern as they looked, outlawed Christmas and Saint Nicholas [SAINT GAUDENS STATUE].

From the beginning of the Protestant Reformation, leaders had tried to persuade their followers to abandon all practices linked with Catholicism. Since the word *Christmas* literally means "Christ's Mass," it was obvious that it was a holy day in the Catholic calendar. Therefore, Saint Nicholas, gift-giving, and the observance of the day itself were detestable and idolatrous.

In Europe, many clung tenaciously to long-established observances. In the British Isles, however, the Puritans gained the upper hand through military and political victories. Typically stern, Puritans formally banned the observance of Christmas in Scotland, England, and northern colonial America.

According to the Puritans, there were three things wrong with the season long made joyful by Saint Nicholas's visits. It was tainted with popish influences; it perpetuated pagan ideas and practices; and it had been condoned—even encouraged—by the Church of England and the British monarchs, two prime targets of Puritan wrath.

In Scotland, Calvinist reformers defeated Catholics on the battlefield in 1559. Once in power, they enacted legislation that included a ban on celebrating Christmas.

Father Christmas, who for a time replaced the outlawed Saint Nicholas, used pagan symbols [ALFRED CROQUILL].

In Anglican England, a move to "purify" the Church of England gained momentum under the Stuarts who believed in the "divine right" of kings. In 1649 Charles I was beheaded and the Puritan Oliver Cromwell became the "protector" of the commonwealth. The Puritan-controlled Parliament passed legislation forbidding church services and civic festivities on Christmas Day and ordered that the feast of Christmas be abandoned under pain of punishment. In many cities and hamlets, December 24 came to be marked by town criers going about shouting, "No Christmas! No Saint Nicholas!"

Along with Saint Nicholas and his visits, special Christmas foods were outlawed. Mince pie was especially singled out because traditionally this delicacy had been shaped to represent a crib and was adorned with a pastry baby on top. Cromwell made it a criminal offense to eat this "superstitious meat."

Use of Christmas candles was forbidden, also, and it became an offense against the realm to sing carols. Under the Puritan regime, the season was transformed into business as usual, and shops were required by law to remain open on December 25. Even Parliament met in session on Christmas Day.

Unable to continue their traditional Christmas celebrations, the English transformed Saint Nicholas into Father Christmas. No longer bearing any symbol suggestive of Catholicism, the new "spirit of Christmas" was often depicted as wearing a crown of holly. Sometimes he carried a Yule log upon his back, and often he had a wassail bowl in his hands. These made him thoroughly pagan and, hence, less objectionable to the authorities. The image of Father Christmas somehow survived in Britain as late as World War I.

Saint Nick fared much better in the New World, where Dutch settlers popularized him during the eighteenth century. In the early nineteenth century Washington Irving described him so vividly that increasing numbers of Americans began to look forward to his Christmas visits in their homes. Yet it was a specialist in the Hebrew language who elevated the spirit of Christmas to new heights while altering his appearance.

The scholar, Clement C. Moore, died believing that his chief contribution to the world was his book *A Compendious Lexicon of the Hebrew Language,* published in 1810. However, twelve years after it was published, he recited an original poem as a special gift for his four older children on Christmas Eve. Moore spoke the words from memory and did not bother to put them into writing. It was not until forty years later, at age eighty-two, that he was persuaded by the New York Historical Society to provide a handwritten copy of his "A Visit from St. Nicholas."

A British recruitment poster of 1917 showed a Santa still much like Father Christmas.

As depicted by artists in the era before the Civil War, Santa is difficult to recognize today [1848 WOODCUT BY T. C. BOYD].

Tradition handed down through one of his granddaughters says that bells hanging from the neck of his carriage horse suggested "a jolly cadence" to him. As he rode back and forth from his Chelsea House residence to where he worked in New York City, he began making up the verses.

When he called his family together on December 24, 1822, all except the two youngest children sat up with excited interest as their father began reciting:

> 'Twas the night before Christmas,
> when all through the house
> Not a creature was stirring,
> not even a mouse;
> The stockings were hung
> by the chimney with care,
> In hope that St. Nicholas
> soon would be there . . .

Scholar Clement C. Moore [DICTIONARY OF AMERICAN PORTRAITS]

As Moore emphasized his dramatic words with gestures, his beautiful young wife hastily scribbled. The children old enough to understand insisted that they liked "Daddy's poem" and begged to hear it several times during the Christmas season.

When Miss Harriet Butler of Troy, New York, visited the Moores a year later, she happened to see Eliza's copy of her husband's poem and insisted upon making a copy for herself. Back home, she gave it to Orville L. Holley, editor of the *Troy Sentinel,* who published it on December 23, 1823. Editor Holley told readers that "we know not to whom we are indebted" for the vivid lines.

Clement Moore learned of the publication and expressed regret. "I do not want my name attached to these lines," he said. "I have a reputation as a scholar and cannot afford to risk injury to it."

It was not until 1838 that Moore admitted his role publicly. Six years later, he collected all his poems in a slender volume, including the lines still known as "A Visit from St. Nicholas."

Nothing else in his volume has survived, but the popularity of his tribute to Saint Nicholas proved greater than its early admirers could

Clement C. Moore's St. Nicholas was a thoroughly North American Dutch burgher [WOODCUT BY T. C. BOYD].

have anticipated. When it appeared as a sixteen-page booklet in 1848, illustrations by artist T. C. Boyd showed Saint Nicholas looking more like a Dutch burgher than today's Santa Claus.

Although not all artists realized it, Clement Moore had given the world's young in heart a new portrait not remotely like Father Christmas or the grim Saint Nicholas of medieval times. His "spirit of Christmas" rode in a miniature sleigh rather than in a carriage. Lively and quick, he was skillful in handling the reins of eight tiny reindeer whom he called by name:

> Now, Dasher! now Dancer!
> now, Prancer and Vixen!
> On Comet! on Cupid!
> on, Donner and Blitzen!

Dressed from head to foot in fur, Saint Nicholas became "all tarnished with ashes and soot" as he bounded down chimneys. Although the bundle on his back made him appear somewhat like a peddler, he was in no way frightening.

Instead, Moore's Saint Nick was "chubby and plump, a right jolly old elf." Gripping "a stump of a pipe" between his teeth, he bore no resemblance at all to a European Catholic bishop or to the Near Eastern saint of the fourth century.

For the first time, Saint Nicholas was thoroughly North American in appearance and mode of transportation.

A Surprise Public Appearance

"WE WERE SOMEWHAT AMAZED AT A PERsonage who dropped in upon us a night or two ago," the editors of the *New York Herald* informed their readers on December 24, 1864.

According to their lengthy account, the outer door of the editorial office opened suddenly, and a mysterious stranger appeared.

"He had a queer, quaint, and remarkable aspect. A great fur cap of the richest and darkest sable covered his head. An immense greatcoat, trimmed with the same choice fur, reached to his knees. The fur collar of this coat was upturned to cover his face. Long top boots, lined and trimmed with fur, covered his feet. In his hand he carried a black valise."

The visitor found it hard to believe that the newsmen did not know him.

"*Dunder und Blitzen,*" he said. "That's what it is to be a historical personage! You have heard of me. All the world has heard of me, and yet you don't recognize me. I can't believe it! I won't believe it! Look at me!"

The editors scrutinized their visitor but still were perplexed.

"He seemed a little old man, short and stout, with the jolliest red face, a nose set with the carbuncles of generous living, snowy white hair, and tiny bright twinkling eyes full of benevolence and fun. Beneath his greatcoat he wore an old-fashioned jacket opened at the throat to disclose an equally old-fashioned ruffle and decorated at the buttonhole with a sprig of Christmas greens and a cluster of hollies."

When the newsmen admitted their bewilderment, their visitor moved closer to them and cried, "'Bless you! If you can't remember me, I'll introduce myself! My name is Santa Claus, Kriss Kringle, or

Saint Nicholas. How do you do?' And with this, he held out his hand."

The editors confessed to their readers that they were astonished beyond measure. "If our visitor had declared himself to be Hendrik Hudson, tired of playing ninepins and waiting for another Rip Van Winkle among the Kaatskills and on a visit to New York to see the sights of the town, we might perhaps have believed him. But as for Santa Claus—impossible! Evidently this was some mad old gentleman who had escaped his keepers and was out on a masquerade."

❧ "Bless you! If you can't remember me, I'll introduce myself! My name is Santa Claus. . . . How do you do."

To rank and file Americans of the day, the editors' bewilderment was natural and understandable. The secular embodiment of the Christmas spirit was seldom seen by anyone at this Advent season during the Civil War. Santa Claus made mysterious visits to children on Christmas Eve, but he never showed his face. Artists sometimes put sketches of him in newspapers, but public appearances were unheard of.

The reaction of the staff of the *Herald* made it clear to their guest that they considered him to be a lunatic. So he decided to stay a while and talk.

"'Sir,' said the little man, 'I know that it is against the rules of the establishment, but may I smoke?'"

When given a nod of assent, "he drew an old, large meerschaum pipe from his pocket and filled it from an old-fashioned pouch."

Blowing out "an immense cloud of fragrant smoke," he talked freely. "'See, sir, if I had come down this fireplace, you would have believed me to be either Santa Claus or a chimney sweep. If you had caught me busy with your children's stockings in the dead of night, you would have thought me either Kriss Kringle or a burglar.

"'If you had seen me riding over the chimney tops in my sleigh drawn by Prancer and Dancer and the rest of my reindeer, you would have imagined me to be either Saint Nicholas or a passing cloud. But because I walk in at the door like anybody else, you take me for a madman!

"'My dear sirs, do you suppose that because I have lived several centuries I am blind to the progress of the age?

Barely visible (center left), Santa is nearly mobbed at a typical Depression Era appearance.

"'The great, wide chimneys and open fireplaces of olden times were navigable, so to speak. But how could a stout old chap like me get down this narrow chimney or up through those little holes in the floor which you call registers?

"'Now I use the doors or the windows, whichever is the more convenient. And for my sleigh, that is still necessary in some countries. But here the railroads enable me to travel faster.'"

An editor inquired whether "his modern mode of entering houses by the door or windows did not expose him to detection by the children."

"'Not at all,' he replied, 'for the good children are all asleep. And I never visit bad children.'"

Questioned, he explained that he secured his toys from all over the world.

"The pride with which he said this is indescribable. He wielded his pipe like a scepter and looked every inch a king." Yet he was ready—

almost eager—to stress the fact that he was constantly challenged to keep up with change.

"'Changes you see all the while, so my gifts must be changed, too. What will suit a child this year will not suit him next. Often I leave a boy with a top or a hobby horse and find him the next year with a cigar in his mouth. Or I present a little girl with a rag baby, and the next year she is crying for diamond earrings and long skirts.'"

Having listened politely, the editors tossed a question at the man who had come into their offices uninvited. Why, they wondered, did he not closely resemble published sketches?

"'You remark that my portraits do not do me justice,' he responded. 'That must be true, or else I should not have been obliged to introduce myself to you. Still, as very few artists have ever seen me, I cannot wonder at their failures.'"

Santa took time out from greeting adults to pose with small groups of children.

For at least another hour, according to the published report, Santa Claus answered questions and told editors his experiences and views about toys, books, and persons unwilling to cherish illusions ("not fit to be trusted with a sixpence and totally destitute of heart").

Then abruptly wishing his new acquaintances goodbye and "Merry Christmas," he grabbed up his black valise and left.

Stated the editors to their readers: "We heard no footsteps on the stairs, no closing of the door, and saw no one pass out into the silent street. Books and toys upon the table and the notebooks in our hands were the only evidence that he had really been with us.

"The gaslights settled into their steady flame. The fire in the grate fell smouldering into ashes. As we sat down to write this full and true account of the visit of Santa Claus, we could sincerely echo his parting benediction: A Merrie Christmas to you and to all!"

Here, greatly condensed, is the earliest surviving account of a long public visit by Santa Claus. Readers must have shared this classic with their children while wondering that the "spirit of Christmas" would show his face in this way.

Thousands rushed to see Santa when he visited Atlanta, Georgia, in 1934.

Twenty-five years later, department store owner James Edgar of Brockton, Massachusetts, surpassed the editors of the *Herald*. In 1890 he decided to have Santa Claus visit his store and talk with the children.

Edgar himself donned a costume and announced that Santa would be on hand for two hours a day in the late afternoon, after the children were out of school.

He greatly underestimated the public's interest. Before the first week of Santa's visit was concluded, the hours were expanded and a costume was prepared for floor walker Jim Grant so he could be stationed at a second location within the store.

As word of the daily appearances spread, children began pouring into Brockton from nearby towns, and then from Boston by train. By Christmas Eve, America's first department store Santa Claus had been paid homage by youngsters who came from as far away as New York City and parts of Rhode Island and New Jersey.

As late as the Great Depression, public appearances of Santa Claus were usually sponsored by urban newspapers and large department stores. While in a city for a week or ten days, he was likely to visit at least one orphanage to spread cheer. The throngs who waited in line to catch a glimpse of Santa were dominated, not by eager boys and girls, but by their parents and grandparents.

Today, typical children can take their choice from among several Santas who appear days ahead of the holiday to listen to gift lists and have their photographs made with small admirers, for a price. Gone are the days when it was a matter of such rarity for Santa to show his face that a major newspaper would devote several columns to an account of his late-night visit to an editorial office.

The "Father" of Santa Claus

"I LIKE MOST OF THE POEM, BUT SANTA CLAUS looks like he just stepped off a little farm in Holland, Thomas."

"Let me take a look," responded cartoonist Thomas Nast.

He pursed his lips as he read in *Harper's Weekly* a reproduction of Clement C. Moore's handwritten copy of his Christmas poem. Already in 1861 it was considered a classic.

"You are dead right," he told his wife. "The artist either didn't read the poem carefully or didn't care. I suppose I must get busy and turn out a better image."

So Nast prepared sketches illustrating the poem that was beginning to be called " 'Twas the Night Before Christmas," using its first phrase rather than the author's title. Skilled artisans carved new images on blocks of hard wood used to print the story.

Thomas Nast, the "father of Today's Santa" [SELF PORTRAIT, AGE FORTY]

Born in Landau, Germany, the artist came to New York with his family at age six. Years later, his grandson, Thomas Nast St. Hill, declared, "My grandfather grew up on stories and images of the Bavarian Santa, jolly and rotund Pelz-Nicol, so he was never fully satisfied with sketches that showed him as a dour Dutchman."

Young Thomas Nast had only a smattering of formal education. In the few classes he attended, however, he spent much of his time drawing. A teacher who noticed his unusual skill suggested that it might land him a job. Nast acted on the idea and at age fifteen was employed by *Leslie's Illustrated Weekly* newspaper. Four years later, he shifted to *Harper's Weekly*, where he remained on the staff for nearly thirty years.

Sent to Civil War battlefields by his editors, Nast turned in sketches that brought the conflict into the homes of Americans throughout Union territory. Later he spent much time crusading against the Tammany Hall political machine of New York's notorious William M. Tweed. When Tweed fled the country, a Nast cartoon caught the eye of a customs agent who spoke no English but recognized the fugitive and placed him under arrest.

However, the most famous political cartoons he created depicted the Republican elephant and the Democratic donkey, symbols still very much alive.

Thomas Nast drew a faceless, money-grubbing Tammany Hall politician shaped much like Santa Claus.

It was Santa Claus that captured Nast's imagination as an artist. "My Santa Claus is better than any previously executed," he told his wife when it appeared in print. "But I am far from satisfied with it. Next year I shall make some improvements."

That resolution launched Nast upon a twenty-five-year search for

When Santa visited a Federal camp during the Civil War, Nast drew him wearing a jacket made from a flag.

"just the right Santa Claus." Annually, he produced numerous new sketches, not all of which were published at the time. Almost every year he introduced a new trait or modified an old one.

His 1862 sketch depicting Santa Claus in a Federal military camp was unusual only by virtue of the setting. Soon, though, he discarded "the stump of a pipe" described by Clement C. Moore. In lieu of this old-fashioned device, he placed a delicate, long-stemmed pipe between Santa's lips.

Under Thomas Nast's skilled pen, Santa Claus took on an entirely new appearance. Sometimes sketched in what looked like old-fashioned winter underwear, Santa eventually donned a suit with a wide belt over his expanding stomach and trimmings of fur. Although published in black and white, the accompanying text often specified that the suit was red and trimmed in white.

Under Nast's hand, Clement C. Moore's "eight miniature reindeer" gradually grew to full size over the years. He liked to depict

Thomas Nast produced a Santa who looked not at all like the cartoonist.

It was Thomas Nast who invented Santa's North Pole headquarters.

them pulling Santa and his sleigh high in the air, with Santa gracefully waving his long-stemmed pipe as he made his departure.

Until Nast pondered the story for several years, no one had given serious thought to Santa's permanent residence. "It is the North Pole!" he cried one day, turning from his drawing board in exultation. "I've found where Santa lives! He spends most of his time in a workshop there and comes out only in time to distribute toys to girls and boys."

Some early Nast sketches showed Santa in what looks much like old-fashioned underwear.

According to the artist, in his North Pole workshop Santa personally put together a stout wooden box with a slot in the top designed for letters from children. Sometimes he worked very late, recording in huge books their names and behavior, information parents were duty-bound to supply him.

Far from being a fixed, static figure, Santa as depicted by Thomas Nast changed with the times. By the time the telephone was more than a rare curiosity, Santa installed one at the North Pole so he could take calls from children who changed their minds after submitting written "wish lists" to him.

Sketches prepared in 1881 are now considered classics. In them Santa Claus is a white-bearded, pot-bellied old gentleman with a merry twinkle in his eyes. Having gradually evolved from the gnome-like Santa described by Clement C. Moore, the figure shaped by Nast has survived for a century without significant changes.

Haddon Sundblom, a commercial artist, made slight modifications of the Nast Santa for the 1931 Christmas season. No longer using a pipe of any kind, the ruddy, jolly Santa who appeared on billboards and in magazines and newspapers that season was sipping Coca-Cola. In spite of the commercial emphasis, Sundblom's Santa was even more eye-catching than Nast's 1881 figure.

During the years that have followed, there have been no more lasting changes in Santa's appearance. In every American city and town, every shopping mall and most department stores annually play host to a Santa who—except for the absence of Coca-Cola and the presence

As depicted in 1881, Santa was rotund, jolly, and loaded with toys.

Santa Claus was one of the first celebrities to be depicted using the telephone.

of cameras—seems to have stepped from the pages of magazines issued in 1931.

In the emerging Space Age, an occasional artist depicts Santa Claus as using a rocket or some other vehicle esigned for extraterrestrial travel. Yet most stick to Moore's eight reindeer, no longer tiny, thanks to Thomas Nast.

One member of the reindeer team has undergone radical change as a result of an advertising campaign by the Montgomery Ward Company. In 1939 the giant mail order retailer bought the idea of publishing in pamphlet form a set of verses written by Robert L. May, who had spent months developing the story of a reindeer named Rudolph. Born with a huge, shiny nose, this little fellow was the butt of practical jokes by other reindeer. They ceased to laugh, however, when Santa sent an urgent message asking for Rudolph's help during a Christmas season when fog made it difficult for him to guide his sleigh. Issued as a giveaway promotion piece with thirty-nine illustrations, 2,500,000 copies of "Rudolph, the Red-nosed Reindeer" were distributed in 1939.

"Rudolph, the Red-Nosed Reindeer," made his 1939 appearance by courtesy of the Montgomery Ward Company.

Seven years later the paperbound booklet was issued in a new edition of 3,500,000 copies. Multitudes of Americans smiled or laughed with delight at the verse of Robert L. May and the illustrations of Denver Gillen, but it took a song writer and a western singer to give Rudolph a permanent place in the lore of Christmas.

Johnny Marks was so impressed by the story of Rudolph that he composed a song featuring him. He first offered the song to Bing Crosby, who rejected the idea of recording it. Gene Autry, next to consider the song, was not very impressed, either. But at the urging of his wife, he agreed to record it. Upon its release, the Autry record was a spectacular success and made Rudolph a perennially favorite American animal.

It was "Rudolph, the Red-nosed Reindeer" that President Richard M. Nixon joyfully thumped out on the piano every Christmas he spent in the White House. Queried, he explained that he used it because it was the first holiday song his daughters Tricia and Julie learned to sing.

Whether guided by Rudolph or making their way without his help, the faithful reindeer annually pull a heavily loaded sleigh from the North Pole. And thus Santa—partly shaped by childhood memories of Bavaria's Pelz-Nicol—now distributes gifts to children of all ages throughout the Western world.

Part Three
O Tannenbaum!

Centuries after Saint Nicholas came to embody the spirit of Christmas giving, peasants of rural Germany began decorating trees at the holiday season. Although the custom survived in limited scope, it took the efforts of prominent individuals to make the Christmas tree a standard part of the season. A queen of England and her husband, as well as presidents of the United States, played prominent roles in this development.

Prince Albert's Splendid Tree

"I HAVE SOMETHING THRILLING TO TELL YOU."

"What is it? A special performance of another play as a Christmas gift?"

"Nothing at all like that," Queen Victoria responded. "While you were away, an artist from the *Illustrated News* spent two entire days here. He made an elegant sketch of your splendid Christmas tree, and it will be published soon."

"Wonderful! I hope it will bring joy to many of your subjects."

"Perhaps. But far more important, it may cause more of them to think favorably of you. Perhaps even like you."

Queen Victoria, who chose Prince Albert as her consort.

That conversation between Queen Victoria and her husband, Prince Albert, shortly before Christmas 1848 shows little awareness of the impact the publication of the artist's sketch of Albert's Christmas tree would have. The story begins years earlier.

Albert first became acquainted with Victoria, the granddaughter of King George III, during adolescence. Long before meeting her, he learned that she was his first cousin and that she was "plump as a partridge." Although he found her less vivacious than he had hoped, still, she was in the line of accession to the throne of England.

King Leopold I of Belgium made no secret of his hope that a match might be arranged between Albert and Victoria, his niece and his nephew. Another of Victoria's uncles, William IV of England, had other ideas. He believed it would be well for the young woman to take Prince Alexander of Orange as her mate.

Following the sudden death of William IV—great-grandson of George I—nineteen-year-old Victoria was crowned in June. Four months later cousin Albert visited her at Windsor Castle.

Writing to her uncle, King Leopold, Victoria had expressed doubts about his protegé. "Though all the reports of Albert are most favorable and though I have little doubt that I shall like him, still one can never answer beforehand for feelings.

"I may not have the feeling for him which is requisite to ensure happiness. I may like him as a friend, and as a cousin, and as a brother, but not more; and should this be the case (which is unlikely) I am very anxious that it should be understood that I am not guilty of any breach of promise, for I never gave any."

Prince Albert as a young man

King Leopold and others tried to sway the queen. Albert, Alexander, and other eligible males attempted to win her affection, but the choice was Victoria's.

In November 1839 Victoria called the eighty-three members of her Privy Council to Buckingham Palace, where she announced her decision to marry Albert. The meeting was a tense one because England had no clear precedent for her to follow. No earlier queen had taken a mate outside the reigning dynasty, and Victoria was adamant that Albert must be made a peer of the realm. And he must be given the title of Prince Consort.

"Your people do not understand me because I am from Germany," Albert told his bride repeatedly. "They think I am like your grandfather, who ruled the nation but never learned to speak English.

"I am entirely different from him. I have found a splendid tutor who will come here every week and teach me the laws and constitution of England. Once I have mastered these matters, I implore you to spend evenings with me reading together *The Constitutional History of England.*"

Queen Victoria refused to promise. Unlike her intellectual husband, she was absorbed with matters of court and etiquette. Albert rode well and shot well, but he had little interest in entertainment. His bride-to-be, on the contrary, danced until 4:00 A.M. on her nineteenth birthday. Before long, the entire realm rejoiced that Victoria had given birth to a male heir. Partly to celebrate the child's arrival, Albert managed to smuggle into the castle a "German surprise" for their Christmas celebration. It was an elegant fir tree decorated with

Americanized version of tree Prince Albert decorated for Queen Victoria.

candles and baubles. Long established in Germany, the practice of setting up Christmas trees was a novelty in England.

"It is right and proper to enjoy it here," Prince Albert insisted. "Your subjects cheat only themselves when they refuse to adopt the Christmas tree. It was Boniface himself (an English missionary known as the Apostle to Germany) who first decorated a fir at Christmas. In the eighth century, he erected it to replace the sacred oak of Odin, at which pagans had offered sacrifices for centuries."

Victoria initially took little interest in the "German tree." However, the following year, one of "Prince Albert's trees" was set up for each of their two children, and soon the holiday season saw the addition of a special Christmas tree for the queen, the largest and most elaborate of all at Windsor Castle.

In 1848 editors of the *Illustrated London News,* one of the most influential newspapers in the Western world, became keenly interested in "Prince Albert's tree." It was a time of great tension in Britain, due to the forces that produced the Crimean War. Many of the queen's subjects still distrusted Victoria's husband and rumors were spread that he had been imprisoned in London Tower as a Russian spy or as an Austrian agent.

What better way to dispel ugly gossip, and perhaps win a few friends for Albert, than by informing the people of his lovely "German custom"?

Windsor Castle was the scene of a Christmas production of *The Merchant of Venice,* part of the revival of English drama under Prince Albert's leadership. The scenery had hardly been taken away before artists appeared to sketch Prince Albert's tree.

The drawing occupied an entire page in a special Christmas supplement published by the newspaper. Even members of the British aristocracy who sneered that Prince Albert was "far too intellectual" suddenly became interested in erecting Christmas trees for their own children.

Sara Josepha Hale, the pioneer woman editor of America's *Godey's Lady's Book,* put her own artist to work just two years after the large picture of Albert's tree was published in London. Hale's artists revised the British sketch by taking out boxes of German biscuits and miniature furniture made from the antlers of stags. To make the tree thoroughly acceptable in a democracy, they carefully removed Queen Victoria's crown as well.

A few Americans had seen Christmas trees earlier through the influence of Hessian mercenaries who fought for the British during the American Revolution. But most readers of the magazine for women had never seen anything even remotely like "Prince Albert's tree" until it appeared in *Godey's* in 1850.

Suddenly given prominence in the English-speaking world on both sides of the Atlantic, the "German custom" of using elaborately decorated trees as central symbols of Christmas became anglicized. Within decades, trees resembling those set up at Windsor Castle by Prince Albert became commonplace in homes on both sides of the Atlantic Ocean.

A Surprise for the First Lady

"WILLIAM, I'VE BEEN DOING SOME SERIOUS thinking. This will be our last holiday season together and our last in the White House. Do you think it might cause Mrs. Pierce to cheer up a bit if we were to bring a Christmas tree into the place?"

President Franklin Pierce took risks for the sake of his disconsolate wife [BRADY STUDIO PHOTOGRAPH, NATIONAL ARCHIVES].

"Interesting thought. Use of these trees is spreading, I think, especially in the Northeast. But as far as I know, there never has been one here. You're thinking about the future, I suppose, when you return home?"

"Yes. Mrs. Pierce has been greatly sheltered in this house. She has improved. You know that, of course. But I'm not sure what a change will do to her. During the last few weeks, she seems to be writing more letters than ever and spending more time in her room."

William D. Snow of New Hampshire, steward, longtime friend, and informal chief of staff to President Franklin Pierce, nodded assent. "I've noticed it, too," he agreed. "But it is just possible that a Christmas tree could upset her rather than help her. How about letting me talk with some of the others before you make a decision?"

"Good idea. Sidney is very sharp. I respect his judgment particularly. But don't overlook Thomas."

Sidney Webster, confidential secretary to the president, had known Mrs. Pierce since the days when he read law in her husband's office. His initial reaction to the president's proposal was cautious.

"On the surface, it sounds great. But it could do more harm than good. Two or three times a week, Mrs. Pierce hands me long letters addressed to Bennie. I always thank her and promise to get them in the mail right away."

"I know there was an accident," Snow commented, "but I never learned the details. What really happened?"

"Mr. Pierce had already been elected to the presidency. Maybe as a sort of final celebration, they went to her parents' home in Concord. They stayed there well into the new year, then headed back home by way of Boston.

"Somewhere between Andover and Lawrence, there was a train wreck. Some say that the axle of a passenger car broke. Whatever the cause, most of the cars were thrown off the tracks down a steep embankment.

At age nine Bennie was photographed with his mother.

"Mr. and Mrs. Pierce were not seriously injured, and as soon as the cars stopped moving, he began looking for their eleven-year-old son Bennie.

"He was their only surviving child, you know. Two other boys had died in infancy, so Bennie was the apple of his mother's eye.

"Mr. Pierce realized that he was badly bruised himself as soon as he began moving. But he hobbled down the hill, searched through the wrecked cars, and found his son. Bennie was pinned under a steel beam, his head crushed."

"I knew it was terrible," Snow commented, "but I had never heard the details. I suppose that's why Mrs. Pierce didn't come here when the president was inaugurated?"

"That's right," Webster continued. "Once she took a look at Bennie's mangled face, Mrs. Pierce said she wanted nothing to do with Washington, D.C. She stopped in Boston and would not leave for several days. Some friends persuaded her to proceed, but she got off the train in Baltimore and found a hotel. She stayed there for several weeks. The president visited her overnight as frequently as he possibly could.

"Once he persuaded her to come to the White House, she had Tom O'Neil unpack all the crepe he could find. Staterooms were draped in black in honor of Bennie, and she picked out two rooms on the second floor and secluded herself in them. She refused to take part in the functions that seem to be mandatory around here and spent much of her time writing letters to Bennie. That is why the president brought Abby here."

"All that happened before I arrived. I wondered why Mrs. Means was acting as official hostess for the White House."

"Abby Means is Mrs. Pierce's aunt, you know, and they were friends in childhood. I think the president was as much concerned about a companion for his wife as for a White House hostess.

"Mrs. Pierce seemed to improve gradually, but as you know she kept up an almost fanatical zeal for the Sabbath. That's why the new concerts by the Marine Band—inaugurated by the president—were moved from Saturday night to Wednesday night. She said the music and revelry prevented her from making proper meditations."

"I think I have heard that story before," Snow replied. "But it's that sort of thing that makes me wonder whether it would be wise to surprise her with a Christmas tree, especially since there has never been one here."

"Anything the president does, or does not do, can trigger another period of depression, I'm afraid. But under the circumstances, I rather incline to support his proposal. It can do little harm. She's bad enough already. And it might do a little good. But before we do anything, I think we ought to consult French. He has had a great deal of experience."

Mrs. Jane Pierce was in "perpetual mourning" for her son Bennie [JOHN C. BUTTRE ENGRAVING].

In the aftermath of the conversation, Sidney Webster went to his assistant, who at age fifty-three was nearly twice his age. A seasoned patent lawyer, Benjamin Brown French was a relative latecomer to the White House staff whose advice had come to be valued highly.

French listened carefully, jotting a few lines on a pad in the methodical fashion for which he was noted.

"It would involve some risk, of course," he concurred. "But I have read that some physicians have had success with victims of melancholy by sudden surprises that seem to shock them out of their condition, at least temporarily.

"If we're going to consider the use of a tree for the Pierces' last Christmas in the White House, why not go a step beyond and bring in a band of children? By keeping the entire enterprise a secret, it would give Mrs. Pierce a great surprise. I'm positive that the boys and girls of the Sunday school would be delighted to come and sing carols. And she probably would recognize some of their faces."

President Franklin Pierce was a brigadier-general during the Mexican War.

Consulting with Franklin Pierce several times about details, his assistant made plans for the surprise. As a result, on the morning of Christmas Eve the president's grieving wife—resisting somewhat and asking questions that were not answered—was led downstairs by her husband to the door of the East Room. As the door opened, children from the New York Avenue Presbyterian Church began singing "Away in a Manger."

Totally surprised, Mrs. Pierce wept so vigorously that she shook: but as she began to regain her composure, her attention was captured by the brightly decorated tree that stood near the middle of the large room. She looked and listened for a long time.

Washington tradition says that Jane Pierce then gave the first radiant smile that anyone in the capital had ever seen on her face.

"Thank you, boys and girls, for your beautiful carols," she said. "Keep your places, please, while Mr. Snow goes to see what sweetmeats Cook has made ready for your visit."

Turning to the president and still radiant with surprise and joy, she embraced him and exclaimed, "Thank you, Mr. Pierce, for the most wonderful Christmas tree in the world. Best of all, Bennie is looking down from heaven and is enjoying it with us. That means I won't even have to write him a letter to describe it! Thank you for the most wonderful Christmas surprise I ever had!"

The President Changed His Mind

Outdoorsman and nature lover Roosevelt tried to persuade Americans not to use Christmas trees.

"MAY WE BE EXCUSED?"

"Both of you have finished your breakfast. There's no special reason for you to stay. But what important business is afoot so early in the morning?"

"We promised to meet Henry."

"Archie, you know better than to refer to Mr. Pinkney as Henry. He may be a waiter, but he is a grown man and you must treat him with respect."

"All right. But we need to go, please."

Turning to ten-year-old Quentin, three years Archie's junior, Theodore Roosevelt demanded, "Since your brother won't talk, perhaps you will tell me what important business you two have with Mr. Pinkney."

"We have to meet him in the Rose Garden."

"Well, that is interesting! When did you boys develop an interest in roses?"

Quentin swallowed hard, looked toward Archie for help that was not forthcoming, and blurted, "It's not roses. It's about a tree."

No longer casual, his father leaned across the breakfast table. "Look me straight in the eyes, Quentin, and tell me what makes this tree so important."

"It's a little cedar tree, just about as tall as my head. Henry—Mr. Pinkney—showed it to us the other day, and he said he thought it was about right for a Christmas tree. He said that if we would meet him in the Rose Garden, he would bring a saw and we could cut it down."

Seldom at a loss for words, Theodore Roosevelt remained silent as he stared directly at his youngest son. After heaving a sigh, the president spoke rapidly and firmly.

Archie and Quentin, standing beside their father, were young enough to demand and get special attention.

"Now, boys, both of you know my rule: no Christmas trees, whether we are at Oyster Bay or here. Archie, you should be ashamed to let your little brother get into trouble. How many years have you heard me say, 'Don't dare to bring a Christmas tree into my house'?"

"As long as I can remember. Maybe about six or seven years."

"And tell your brother exactly why you have always been forbidden to cut trees at Christmas or any other season."

Grimacing as though he wished to make a mocking face at his father but didn't dare to do so, Archie solemnly recited, "Trees are part of nature. Men and women and boys and girls are part of nature, too. We must not abuse nature. Instead of cutting trees down, we should plant them.

". . . That's right, isn't it, Father?"

"Of course that's right, my boy. Now one of you run down the stairs, find Mr. Pinkney, and tell him that there will be no tree cutting, by your father's strict orders.

"Besides, you boys know perfectly well that your Aunt Anna has made plans to give you a splendid Christmas party in just a few days. That should more than make up for the absence of a tree.

"When you boys grow up, you will be proud of your father. A great many Americans look to their president for leadership, and I am happy to learn that some of them have stopped using Christmas trees. Twenty years from now, or thirty, we will have a better nation because there will be more trees."

When informed that a veteran forester advocated cutting small trees at Christmas, Theodore Roosevelt laughed at himself and changed his mind.

Archie nodded understanding and obedience, then went to inform the White House waiter who had taken a special interest in the boys that there was no need to get a saw from the tool shed.

Faithful to her promise, Anna Roosevelt reached Washington in time to make plans for her two small nephews and their sister Ethel. To their surprise and delight, she gave them what she called a "Christmas tree party" in which napkins were imprinted with tiny trees and the tip of a real tree—about fourteen inches in height—was decorated with miniature ornaments.

In the aftermath of their aunt's surprise party, Archie and Quentin are believed to have made secret plans for the following year. At least, that is the tradition preserved by the Roosevelt household staff.

Regardless of when the plans were made, the boys carefully avoided attracting their father's attention as the holiday season approached. On a bright, moonlit night they slipped out of the mansion and went directly to the cedar they had spoken of a year earlier. Cut to stand about three feet high, their little Christmas tree was smuggled up the service stairway and carefully lifted into position in Archie's room.

Quentin Roosevelt astride a favorite pony.

A few days before the end of December, their father learned of the deception and called the boys to his office. After giving them a stern lecture about doing lasting damage to nature by using Christmas trees, he sent them to the nearby office of an official whose judgment he trusted. Since the label *conservationist* had not yet entered general use, Gifford Pinchot habitually called himself a "good friend of Mother Nature."

Given advance notice by Roosevelt of the reason for the boys' visit, Pinchot listened attentively to their story. Then, to their complete surprise, he walked around his desk and sat in a chair close to theirs.

"Tell your father that you came to see me today," he instructed them, "and then tell him that Mr. Pinchot says he is wrong."

"Why?" Archie managed to gasp.

"Because in the National Forest Service, we have found that careful cutting of little Christmas trees helps the big trees. When some of the little ones are taken out, the big ones are not so crowded. You can understand that, can't you?"

Both boys nodded.

"As president of the United States, your father will be doing Mother Nature a good turn by encouraging folk to put trees into their homes every Christmas. In spite of his influence, some of our forestry experts think the use of Christmas trees is growing, not declining. If it ever becomes standard to cut and decorate little trees for the holidays, many of us believe that farmers will begin to grow them as a crop."

"I don't think I can tell Father about that. I don't understand what you mean," Archie interposed.

Gifford Pinchot pulled on the handle of a big map, rolled it down, and pointed toward the Appalachian Mountains.

The White House about the time of Theodore Roosevelt's first term.

"This is one of the regions I'm talking about. You boys have been in the mountains with your parents, I know. Maybe you didn't notice, but there are lots of places where the ground is not level or fertile enough for ordinary crops. But land like that will some day be planted with seedling trees. After six or eight years, they will be big enough for use at Christmas, and people will cut them down, sell them like they sell apples and corn, and then plant more trees in the places where they were cut.

"Now do you understand what I mean by saying that lots of people will run Christmas tree farms some time in the future?"

"Yes, sir!" the boys laughed in delighted unison.

Back at the White House and nearly breathless from running with their message, the brothers persuaded their father's private secretary that they must see him on urgent business. When they told him of their visit to Pinchot and of his belief that cutting trees helped the forests instead of hurting them, Theodore Roosevelt thumped Archie and Quentin on their backs.

Quentin and Archie (right) joined the White House guards for roll call.

"Bully for you, boys! Bully!" he exclaimed. "You two are cut from the same cloth as your father! You didn't take no for an answer before you consulted with an expert.

"Next year, you won't have to smuggle a tree into the house. Maybe we can put one in the Green Room, downstairs, where some of our visitors can enjoy it with us. You boys have made me change my mind. I will begin encouraging people to use Christmas trees."

Reflecting upon the report his sons brought him, the lover of nature shook his head in bewilderment. "I can imagine a day when nearly every American home will have a Christmas tree in it for the holiday season," he mused. "But for the life of me, I can't conceive of anybody trying to raise Christmas trees as a crop."

The White House Led the Way

"MR. PRESIDENT," VETERAN WHITE HOUSE staff member Ike Hoover announced with a flourish that was familiar to old-time Washington insiders, "two members of your cabinet are here to see you."

"I do not have a cabinet," Calvin Coolidge snapped. "I have inherited the cabinet of President Harding. But who are these gentlemen?"

"Secretary Hubert Work of Colorado and Secretary Henry C. Wallace of Iowa. They insist that they have important business to discuss with you."

"I cannot imagine what Interior and Agriculture have in common," fumed the former vice president who had become the nation's chief executive upon the sudden death of Warren G. Harding. Having taken the oath of office just a few days earlier and not yet having held a formal cabinet meeting, Coolidge shook his head in bewilderment and reluctantly said, "All right."

Warren G. Harding, whose death forced Calvin Coolidge to light the first National Christmas Tree.

Once Work and Wallace were in Coolidge's office, the secretary of the interior began to speak. "We have come together because we represent strong common interests. Protection of our national forests is part of my job, and Mr. Wallace must always keep the interests of farmers in mind."

"What has that to do with me?" demanded the new president.

"Long before President Harding's untimely death, we had made plans to come to the Oval Office together. You understand, I hope, that we are simply representing a great many of our—I should say your—constituents.

"That means we are jointly speaking for the American Forestry Commission and its members throughout the nation. These folks are convinced that the time has come to prepare and light a National

Christmas Tree. You know the old saying, 'As Washington goes, so goes the country.'"

"I know the saying," Coolidge conceded. "But what does that have to do with what you are advocating?"

"Excuse the interruption," Secretary of Agriculture Wallace interposed, "but I think I can shed a little light on this matter.

Grace Coolidge

"Americans look to their president for guidance on small issues as well as big ones. There was a period—during the administration of Theodore Roosevelt—when his example caused many families to abandon the long-established custom of erecting Christmas trees."

"That was twenty years ago," Coolidge muttered.

"Yes, Mr. President. And in the intervening twenty or so years, use of Christmas trees has become widespread. So many trees are needed every year that seedlings cut in our national forests will not meet the demand. Many members of the American Forestry Association are now Christmas tree farmers, and they would like to have your help in persuading citizens not to go into the woods with axes or saws in search of suitable trees."

"You mean, they want people to buy the trees they grow, instead of using the ones nature has provided?"

"Yes. But the matter is not that simple. In addition to the damage done to forests when amateurs select trees to be cut, we have good evidence that a number of forest fires have been started by persons wanting to dress up their homes for the holidays.

"Members of the Forestry Association think—and I must say that Mr. Work and I agree with them—that in the long run increased reliance upon Christmas trees planted, tended, and cut for the market will benefit our forests and the nation."

"When I was a boy in Vermont," Coolidge mused, "observance of Christmas was a sacrament. We exchanged gifts, of course, but two weeks earlier we went into the woods and cut a well-shaped spruce. Then we decorated it before the stockings were hung by the chimney."

"Admirable practices, indeed," agreed the secretary of agriculture. "But only a few of our citizens have the privilege of living in the hills of Vermont. Some spend their entire lives in cities. Unless a man is fortunate enough to be able to buy a Christmas tree, he may have little or no contact with living trees, such as you had every day when you were growing up."

"Then let's do something about it!" Coolidge said.

"Splendid! It is now August, and Christmas seems a long time away. But if we are to do this thing properly, we must have time to prepare for it," Hubert Work responded.

"Your predecessors in office have had numerous Christmas trees inside the mansion, but to my knowledge these have been private affairs. We're talking now about a tree of some size, situated on the grounds where it can be seen by the public and launched, so to speak, with a suitable ceremony."

"I think I am to press some buttons to light a Christmas tree on the Ellipse."
— Calvin Coolidge

"That means it will require electric lights, of course," Henry Wallace interposed.

"Yes, brightly colored lights of some power," Work nodded. "What would you think of bringing a suitable tree from Vermont, Mr. President?"

"I would like that, but would it come from a tree farm?"

"I am afraid not. Commercially grown trees are usually harvested when they are six to eight feet tall, not nearly large enough to be national symbols. For what we have in mind, a splendid native tree will be selected, shipped here, and erected at a prominent spot. But this tree, ceremonially lighted by the president of the United States, will provide an occasion for suggesting to our citizens that they purchase trees grown for this purpose."

Thus the first National Christmas Tree came to be cut from a Vermont forest late in November 1923.

Although the event excited public interest as soon as plans were announced, the Coolidge family had two additional trees for themselves. A large tree was set up in the Blue Room, and a much smaller one was erected in the upstairs bedroom of the Coolidge boys.

While agreeable to the idea from the first, President Coolidge was less than enthusiastic as time passed. On December 21 he confided to

President and Mrs. Coolidge with their pet dog Rob Roy.

his diary: "I don't know as I have any very definite plans for Christmas. I believe there is a plan for a church service, a union service, which I think is to be held in the church that I attend, on Christmas morning, where I expect to go. And I think I am to press some buttons to light a Christmas tree on the Ellipse."

In spite of Coolidge's hesitancy, the idea of the National Christmas Tree evoked enthusiastic reactions from writers, photographers, editors, and publishers. Few newspapers in the nation failed to give space to the innovation, and some magazines treated the ceremonial lighting as a national milestone of great importance.

Like many other ceremonies, the lighting of the National Christmas Tree in Washington eventually became a ritual. Except during times of war or national emergency when the symbolic tree remained dark or was lighted only briefly, it has been so widely accepted that no chief executive has questioned its propriety.

Enshrined at the center of the nation's power base, the once-rare Christmas tree now receives almost universal homage in homes of Americans of various ethnic and most religious backgrounds. Even in cities and towns where court rulings have outlawed manger scenes and related imagery from public property, the custom of erecting and decorating a Christmas tree usually remains hale and hearty.

Part Four

First Achievements and Events

The background and origin of some things linked with Christmas are obscure and cannot be traced clearly. Others are surprisingly well documented. While the holiday season has too many notable "firsts" for the subject to be treated exhaustively, many are so striking that they have long since become part of the celebration of Christmas.

The First Christmas Card

"JOHN, I AM GRATEFUL FOR YOUR COURTESY IN responding to my message. I know you are busy, but I wonder if you might be interested in a novelty?"

"That would depend, Sir Henry. The prime minister has been urging me to pursue the idea of designing and executing a mural for the House of Lords."

"Splendid! I will put in a good word for you at every opportunity. But you know how slowly the wheels of government move. Even if it is approved, it will be a twelvemonth before you will be allowed to start. My novelty will not interfere with such a project. You can prepare a sample for me in a matter of days."

"Precisely what do you have in mind?"

Sir Henry Cole, a wealthy long-time civil servant with a passionate interest in fine art, leaned back in his chair and became expansive.

"My many interests are troubling me. Here it is already August, and I have suddenly realized that I shall have to extend two or three hundred greetings at the Christmas season," Cole explained.

"You plan to pen brief messages on calling cards and leave them at the doors of your friends, I assume?"

"That is what I have always done, and all London with me. But it occurs to me that a printed card with a suitable design could be sent through the penny post. It would save me a great deal of time, and I believe the recipients would be surprised and delighted."

Artist John Callcott Horsley, destined to be elected to the prestigious Royal Academy of Art only a few years later, nodded in agreement. "The concept is novel. So novel that it might very well prove to be the talk of the city. But," he suggested, "since you are considering printing them for your personal use, why not produce twice as many and offer them for sale in your Bond Street shop?"

"A splendid suggestion, indeed!" Cole responded. "Why did I not think of it myself? People who come to Bond Street seeking objects for decorating the home should be willing to spend a shilling on a decorated card to replace those calling cards that all look alike, sterile and black and white."

"What do you wish me to do, Sir Henry?"

"Go back to your studio and prepare a sketch, perhaps three inches high and five inches wide. It ought to be suitable for hand coloring after it is printed, and it should have scenes suitable for the Christmas season. If I like it—and I am sure that I shall—I know just the right man to put such a design into the press."

Horsley's initial design, submitted one week after talking with Sir Henry Cole, was modified only slightly for the printer. Three panels, tiny as they were, constituted what the artist insisted upon calling a triptych.

Vine-wrapped boughs formed frames for the three scenes. At the left, a benevolent citizen was busy at the traditional Christmas activity of feeding the hungry. Another tiny sketch at the right portrayed the act of clothing the naked. The center section, which was

Sir Henry Cole's 1843 Christmas card represented a radical innovation.

the largest, contained a happy family of three generations—including a dog—joyfully celebrating the holiday, glasses in hand. A short line at the top and an even shorter one at the bottom were designed for the names of senders and recipients.

Published at Summerly Home Treasury Office, 12 Old Bond Street, London, in 1843, the card was less than a sensational success. Some of the patrons of Cole's shop purchased copies at one shilling each, and Cole himself sent an estimated three hundred through the penny post. About one dozen of these first Christmas cards published for sale are held by collectors today.

Some of those who received the cards were far from pleasantly surprised. They were attracted to Sir Henry Cole's novel idea, but the central panel offended followers of the temperance movement. Denounced as "deliberately conceived to foster and promote the consumption of alcohol during the holiday season," it became the target of considerable verbal abuse.

Although Cole smarted under the attack, he confided to Horsley that the unexpected response had served another purpose.

"You know my deep interest in the penny post," he said. "But you may not know that after it was introduced three years ago, postal revenues dropped."

"That surprises me," Horsley replied. "Did not Mr. Rowland Hill predict a sharp increase in revenue once the new system was in operation?"

"He did, indeed. But he was wrong," Cole explained. "I'm sure you are well acquainted with his pamphlet 'Post Office Reform: Its Importance and Practice.' It's hard to believe it's been out for five years. He was positive that by charging only a penny for half an ounce, regardless of distance, the postal service would thrive."

"How far off the target was he, Sir Henry?"

"During the first year, revenues of the postal service dropped by at least sixty percent. However, the attacks on the Christmas cards we produced have brought a great deal of attention to the penny post. That means they are likely to persuade more of the public to use the postal service instead of delivering their greetings in person. Come next Christmas, we must try again!" Cole insisted.

If their venture was repeated, no cards have survived. A design similar to the 1843 card was used by W. M. Egley of London in 1848, and it is generally considered the second commercially produced Christmas card. It, too, failed to capture the public's imagination.

During the 1860s, members of Britain's royal family began to commission artists to produce special holiday paintings. Reproduced in color and used on Christmas cards, they helped to popularize the cards. Later in the decade, London's Marcus Ward and Company began to employ artists to design Christmas cards. One of them, Kate Greenaway, later became famous as an illustrator of children's books.

Cards for distribution at the New Year had come into vogue centuries earlier. Medieval artists produced many of them by engraving religious scenes and biblical quotations on wooden blocks.

In the United States, handwritten Christmas cards were plentiful by the time of Andrew Jackson. So many of them were sent that the

The second commercially produced Christmas card, London, 1848.

superintendent of mails in Washington, D.C., annually hired extra workers for the holiday season. About 1822, he formally complained to Congress, asking that they pass laws to halt the exchange of Christmas cards by mail.

His petition got nowhere.

Half a century passed before the printed Christmas card became popular in the United States. German-born Louis Prang, who immigrated to America after the revolution of 1848, is credited with opening the American market in 1875.

Prang's early cards, even smaller than those of Sir Henry Cole, reproduced famous works of art. Gradually they expanded until most were seven inches tall and ten inches wide. Elegant lithographs, they sold for one dollar, a price that eventually forced him out of business.

One of Prang's chief distributors, the Gibson Art Company, prospered from his cards during the 1880s. A generation later, its executives persuaded the company to begin producing original designs of their own.

Christmas cards have dealt with almost every idea and object associated with the season, and a few that were not. Victorian cards often were embellished with silk or satin, while depicting holly, robins, stagecoaches, puddings, and mistletoe. Many early American cards featured Santa Claus—barely recognizable today—and a black servant setting the table for the Christmas feast.

Many World War I Christmas cards stressed hugs and kisses, while those of World War II often featured Santa standing by an American flag. Auto-driving Santas and flappers appeared on the cards of the 1920s, and when the world entered the Space Age a series of cards depicted Santa in a space capsule instead of a sleigh.

Perhaps the most unusual of Christmas cards came into vogue in 1880. For much of the decade, dead robins were popular subjects. Scholars theorize that the medieval tradition of slaying a robin or wren during the holidays was the source of this motif. Nevertheless, cards depicting dead robins were successful.

Bells, children, tiny animals, birds, greenery, and Santa Claus are

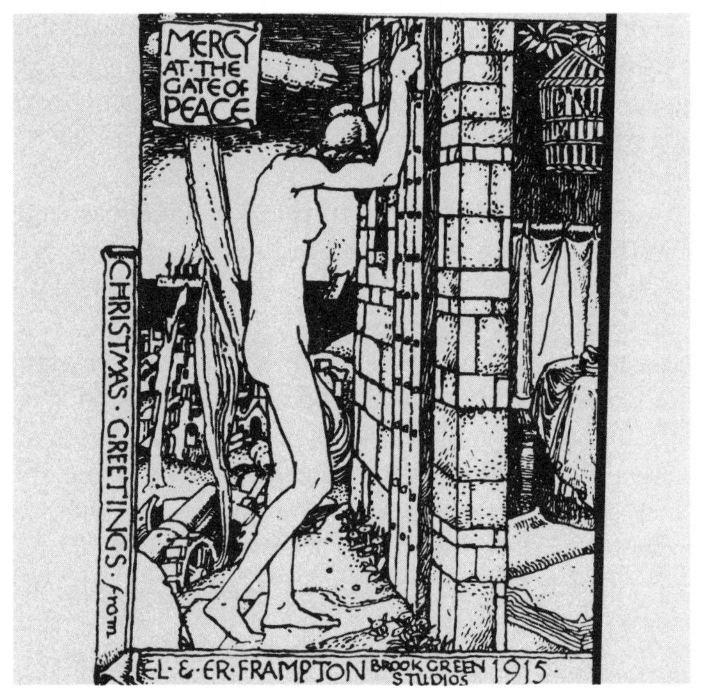

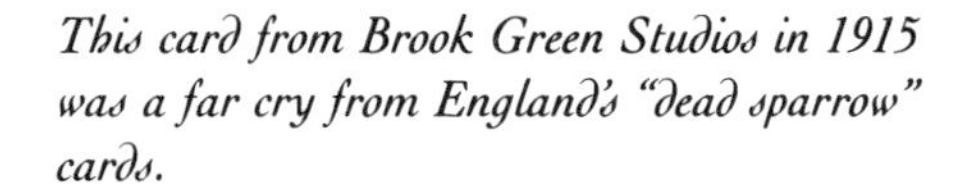
This card from Brook Green Studios in 1915 was a far cry from England's "dead sparrow" cards.

established American favorites. But the most novel card ever printed in the United States can claim no long-neglected holiday tradition. In 1915 a card produced at Brook Green Studios featured a nude woman, discreetly turned ninety degrees away from the viewer!

If Sir Henry Cole's experiment was a failure, it was turned to triumph nearly a century later by Joyce C. Hall of Kansas City, Missouri. With two brothers, Hall imported and sold art cards so successfully that she opened a specialty shop offering cards, stationery, and gift items.

Fire destroyed the Hall inventory in 1915. Instead of quitting, the sister and her two brothers bought an engraving plant and began creating original cards for wholesale and retail distribution. Today, Hallmark offers more than 2,000 different Christmas cards each year. John C. Horsley, who dashed off the one-side design in 1843 at the request of Sir Henry Cole, would be amazed at the enthusiasm with which Christmas cards are now used.

The First Christmas Seal

Danish postal clerk Annoyer Holboell planned the first Christmas seal [AMERICAN LUNG ASSOCIATION].

"WHAT ARE YOU MUMBLING ABOUT, Annoyer?" inquired a Copenhagen, Denmark, postal clerk.

"I'm not mumbling. I'm singing a Christmas song," his colleague replied.

"Doesn't sound like any Christmas song I've ever heard. Are you making a joke?"

"No, indeed. I am not joking. It makes you think I am not singing because I am using words of my own about something new I'm thinking of making."

"You don't really mean something new, do you? You must mean making a change in something old?"

"No, something no one ever made before. Something really new."

"What is it?"

"You will laugh at me if I tell you."

"No, I will not laugh. Please tell me. I would like to know."

Big, good-natured Annoyer Holboell lowered his voice to a confidential level and began hesitantly. "I want to make a stamp," he explained. "A brand new stamp. Not for sending mail. Something to put on a letter alongside the postage stamp."

"Why would anyone want to put something else on a letter?"

"Because lots of persons want to help the children who have tuberculosis. I think they will buy a special stamp that would let people who get their letters know that they have entered the fight to help sick children. I've already talked to our postmaster about it. He likes the idea and says it ought to be tried out this time next year."

Nearly twelve months later, in early December 1904, patrons of the Danish postal service were offered a chance to purchase "Christmas stamps" at one-half penny each. King Christian IX gave his support to Holboell's idea; so the half-penny printed pieces bore a portrait of the late Queen Louise and the word *Julien,* Danish for "Merry Christmas."

So many of the new Christmas stamps were bought that after two seasons, during which people began to ask for "Christmas seals" instead of "stamps," that two new hospitals were built for children who were victims of tuberculosis.

In the first decade of this century, tuberculosis was second only to pneumonia as the cause of death in the Western world. In the United States, ordinary folk often called the disease consumption. Oliver Wendell Holmes insisted upon calling it the "white plague."

One victim, Dr. Edward L. Trudeau, wanted to die in peace and quiet, so he built a cottage at Lake Saranac, New York, and gave up his medical practice. Instead of dying, he improved, and soon he converted his cottage into a two-patient tuberculosis hospital, America's first. This led to the formation of the National Tuberculosis Association in 1904, the year Annoyer Holboell's stamps were first used.

Some of the Danish stamps were put on a package mailed to America, where the noted writer Jacob Riis, who had been born in Denmark, was already interested in tuberculosis. Six of his brothers had died from it, so he wrote suggesting that Americans use Christmas seals to fight the white plague.

In 1904 Emily Bissell of Wilmington, Delaware, remembered the Riis article when she was challenged to help find funding for a tuberculosis shack on the Brandywine River. Her cousin, Dr. Joseph Wales, director of the facility, urged her to do what she could. "We're down to our last dollar," he wrote. "Unless we can somehow find three hundred dollars, the poor patients will have to be sent home to die, and perhaps to spread the disease to others. Please! You've got to help us!"

Responding to Dr. Wales' plea, Emily Bissell designed a seal that incorporated the symbol of the American Red Cross and a half-wreath of holly above the words *Merry Christmas.*

Offered a chance to sponsor sales, Red Cross officials said no, but they did not object to her idea of mentioning the Delaware Red Cross on envelopes in which twenty-five stamps were packaged.

With her plans complete, Emily Bissell went to a printer. To her consternation, she was told that it would cost forty dollars, more money than she had on hand, to produce fifty thousand seals. After two friends lent her the money, the seals were printed and, by permission of the Wilmington postmaster, went on sale in the corridor of the post office on December 7, 1907.

Sold at one cent per package, each envelope containing Christmas seals urged the purchaser to:

> Put this stamp with message bright
> On every Christmas letter;
> Help the tuberculosis fight,
> And make the New Year better.

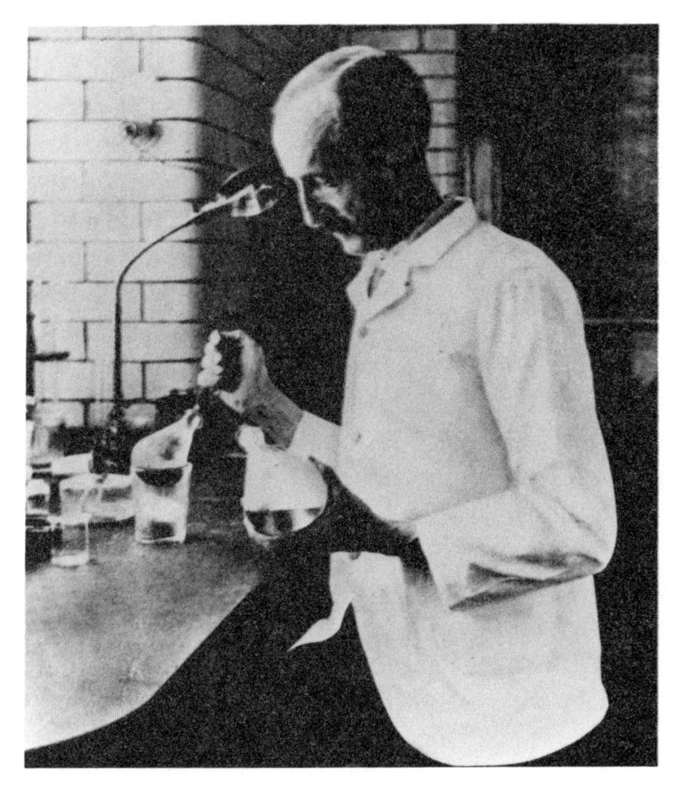

Dr. Edward L. Trudeau went off to die and created a pioneer "tuberculosis shack" [AMERICAN LUNG ASSOCIATION].

Known later as the "mother of Christmas seals in America," Emily Bissell was elated when sales the first day brought in nearly twenty-five dollars. However, interest waned very soon, so she went to the *North American* newspaper. "We must let the people know what is happening," she pleaded, but the editors were not enthusiastic. It seemed inappropriate to them to link the joys of Christmas with the fear of a dreaded disease.

Columnist Leigh M. Hodges, who heard Emily Bissell's plea, persuaded his chief to let him become involved. Publicity and contacts with such notables as Theodore Roosevelt boosted the income from the seals to three thousand dollars, ten times as much as was needed at the Brandywine River shack.

The Wilmington success persuaded American Red Cross officials to sponsor a nationwide campaign in 1908. This time, sales yielded $135,000. Tuberculosis associations soon became involved, and in 1920 they took over the entire program.

Today *Christmas Seals* is a registered term, and the American Lung Association no longer sells seals but distributes them and asks for contributions. Each December, seals are mailed to approximately forty million households, nearly half of those in the nation.

In the United States, new designs are produced annually. For several years, art work from school children of each state and territorial possession was used, which meant that in 1975 and then in 1977 through 1980 the sheets contained fifty-four different designs, now prized collectibles.

At the time Emily Bissell responded to her cousin's urgent plea, tuberculosis claimed the lives of at least 150,000 Americans each year. Funds raised by Christmas Seals have helped establish sanitariums in which patients could be healed, and in 1938 there were 732 such institutions in use. Five years later, Dr. Selmon A. Waksman discovered streptomycin, the first antibiotic to prove effective against tuberculosis.

With tuberculosis no longer the white plague, funds raised through distribution of Christmas Seals in the United States, about forty mil-

Emily Bissell, the "mother of Christmas seals in America" [AMERICAN LUNG ASSOCIATION].

lion dollars annually, go to combat all lung diseases, including cancer, asthma, emphysema, chronic bronchitis, neonatal distress syndrome, and—occasionally—a case of tuberculosis.

At his death in 1927, Annoyer Holboell's portrait was used on the Danish seal. Earlier, he had been knighted and given decorations by several European monarchs. Today the grave of the man who created a novel stamp to combat tuberculosis bears the inscription "Father of the Christmas Stamp."

"Jingle Bells"

"MR. PIERPONT HAS COME HERE FROM CALifornia," the hostess announced after clapping her hands for attention. "Since he was not born among us but has chosen to live here, custom entitles him to a wish.

"Let's all stand in a circle, join hands, and close our eyes. Mr. Pierpont will make a silent wish. After we hear the bell that announces the New Year, he will tell us what he most hopes to receive in 1857."

As the guests of the New Year's Eve party in Savannah, Georgia, listened expectantly, their new friend shook his head in bewilderment. "I've got just about everything a fellow could want," he mused. "But there is one thing. No, two . . ."

"Tell us! Tell us!"

So James Pierpont, the son of Boston's abolitionist Unitarian minister the Reverend John Pierpont, Sr., and brother of Savannah's the Reverend John Pierpont, Jr., began to explain himself.

"I guess the first thing I really want in the New Year is to see something white, besides cotton."

Brief bewilderment was followed by laughter. Savannah was famous as a center of the cotton trade. Mule-drawn wagons loaded with cotton were commonplace, and the streets were littered with lint most days of the year. At the booming Cotton Exchange, the volume of trade was growing so rapidly that Savannah was hoping to overtake London soon as the world's largest cotton market.

"Don't knock cotton! It's our bread and butter," a guest called out. "There's lots more money in cotton than in snow!"

Transplanted Bostonian James Lord Pierpont [COURTESY OF MARGARET W. DEBOLT].

John Pierpont

When the laughter subsided, the hostess spoke for the group. "Your chance of getting your first wish isn't very great, Mr. Pierpont. Maybe you'll do better with the second one. But for it to have a chance to come true, you must tell us what it is."

Grinning, the wanderer who had gone to sea at age fourteen and later had wound up penniless after finding no gold in California cupped a hand behind his ear. "I guess I wish that some time this year I'll hear a bell besides the big one at the Cotton Exchange."

The puzzled looks on the faces of his new acquaintances led him to explain.

"Back where I grew up—not California, but Boston—you can step out on the street any New Year's Eve and hear sleigh bells jingling. I sure do like Savannah. Guess I'll settle down here. But especially on a night like this, I miss the snow and the sleigh bells."

Then he added, "My father writes poems and songs, mostly about freeing the slaves . . ."

The Savannah Cotton Exchange was one of the busiest in the world.

Savannah had elegant coaches and carriages, but not a single sleigh.

"You bring shame on this house by your presence, sir!" a lifelong Savannahan interrupted.

Pierpont did not make a direct reply. Instead, he thought for a moment, then continued. "I have written a few songs myself. But now that I am a Southerner just like the rest of you, my sentiments are with you and not with my father. Lots of folks say we're going to fight. Well, if we do, I will be fighting for the South!

"Right now, though, you've got me wishing I could be out in the snow, listening to bells jingling. Sometimes I hear those bells in my dreams, but I hadn't really thought much about them in a long time. Not until you told me to make a wish for the New Year."

In September 1857 Boston's Oliver Ditson publishing firm issued a song sheet titled "The One Horse Open Sleigh." Since it was credited simply to "J. Pierpont," Bostonians who saw it assumed that it had come from the prolific pen of the Reverend John Pierpont, Sr. In 1859 a new edition of the song was printed, with the title modified to "Jingle Bells, or the One Horse Open Sleigh."

Now a priceless relic, the Cotton Exchange Bell hangs in a building erected to house it.

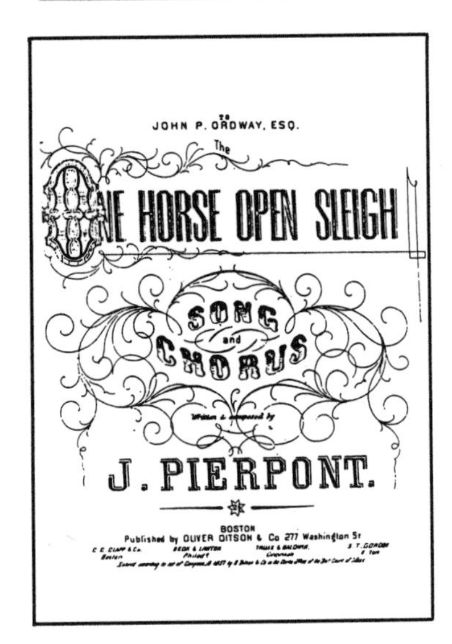

Title page of the first edition of Pierpont's song, then called "The One Horse Open Sleigh."

Called by whatever name, the lines written in snowless Savannah by a rebellious wanderer who was nostalgic for the sights and sounds of his boyhood became immensely popular. Now familiar through an estimated forty arrangements, "Jingle Bells" is widely regarded as a folk song. However, the authorship was established only a few years ago by a study of letters exchanged among members of the Pierpont family.

When the war came, James Pierpont's declaration of unity with his adopted South proved to be true. Having married the daughter of a mayor of Savannah, he saw his brother John to the railroad station to return to Boston, then donned Confederate gray and fought through most of the Civil War as a member of the First Georgia Cavalry.

James Pierpont is buried in the Savannah family plot of his wife, close to the body of a brother-in-law who died at First Bull Run. During the conflict, he composed dozens of ditties and several war songs. In spite of such fervent battle hymns as "We Conquer or Die," "Our Battle Flag," and "Strike for the South!" the Southerner-by-adoption is remembered today only for the rollicking lines of his sleighing song inspired by New Year's Eve memories of his native Boston.

A Penny Saved . . .

"MERKEL, I NEED YOUR HELP."

"Of course, John. Carlisle Trust and I will do anything we can for you."

"Oh, I don't mean personal help. I'm thinking about my employees."

"They're important to the economy of the city. How many do you have working now?"

"The Lindner Shoe Company is proud to provide most or all of the livelihood for about seventy-five families, Merkel."

Merkel Landis, treasurer of the Carlisle Trust Company in Carlisle, Pennsylvania, leaned back in his chair before asking, "Just what are you after, friend? New mortgages? Some type of new loan program?"

"Oh, no! Nothing of that sort!" John Lindner responded. "What I'm looking for is a way to encourage our people to save a little money. By comparison with lots of other industries, they draw good wages. But most of them can't seem to save a nickel."

"One nickel doesn't mean much. Many nickels can mean a lot," the banker mused. "Maybe you have given me an idea. Let me chew on it for a week, and I'll see if I can come up with a plan. How about meeting me for lunch next Wednesday?"

The head of the shoe manufacturing company agreed to his friend's suggestion. The next week they met again, some time in early spring 1909.

"I think I have something for you, John," the banker began. "Everybody I know is strapped for cash at Christmas. The holiday season puts nearly all of us in a bind, but I believe it also can offer an incentive to save. You said something about nickels last week. How about asking your workers to sign up for a Christmas account that will

Dickinson College, Carlisle, Pennsylvania, whose faculty members soon became Christmas Club savers.

give them extra cash at Christmas and cost them only a nickel a week?"

"Sounds interesting," the manufacturer nodded. "How would it work?"

"Carlisle Trust is willing to help you out at no profit. Matter of fact, we all know that this is a year of uncertainty. The income tax amendment is being debated in the Senate right now, and most experts say it is sure to pass. If it does, that means Uncle Sam will be taking a bite out of every paycheck, making it harder than ever to deal with the economic pressures of Christmas.

"I've already drawn up tentative specifications for a Christmas Club savings plan," he continued. "Any employee of yours who signs up by December will have at least $2.60 extra to spend the following Christmas, regardless of what the new income tax does to his paycheck."

"Won't that create a lot of extra traffic for you at the bank, John?"

"No, I don't see it that way at all. If you'll look over my proposal, you'll notice that I am not suggesting small individual weekly deposits. Just make payroll deductions, deposit the entire amount with us, and at Christmas we'll be ready to hand out the cash. Of course, you'll want to arrange to deduct whatever your people say, but I think a nickel a week ought to be the minimum."

"You say it won't cost Lindner Shoe Company anything? That's splendid! But what about interest on the savings?"

"Cost of handling numerous small accounts will be greater than the interest earned from the money. Unless your employees get far beyond the minimum, I don't see any way we can pay interest on a Christmas Club account. But at the very least, it will accomplish the thing you came to see me about: encouragement of personal savings, no matter how small."

"We might get started by offering to take out five pennies a week," Lindner mused. "Folks are beginning to get interested in the new Lincoln head coin that is due to replace the Indian head penny that has been in circulation for fifty years. For employees who want to start your Christmas Club savings plan at the bottom, we could offer to take out five pennies a week. They will be able to come to the bank about the middle of December and get five half-dollars and a dime."

"Getting Ready for Christmas" in the Pennsylvania countryside.

Shaking hands on the plan, Merkel Landis made the necessary arrangements for the new special accounts. John Lindner called his employees together to explain it to them. Neither man anticipated how delighted Lindner Shoe Company employees would be to receive what they called their "Christmas bonus," accumulated through their own savings.

Talk about the plan created so much interest in Carlisle that in 1911 the bank expanded the program. Any person could participate by payroll deduction of a nickel a week or more or by personal deposit.

To the delight of bank employees, some who started their individual Christmas Club savings plans agreed to deposit one dollar each week. A few went beyond that to save enough cash to make a down payment on one of Henry Ford's Model-T automobiles.

American Banker magazine and other specialized publications do not provide complete information about the level of activity in Christmas Clubs today. Of the more than twelve thousand banks in the United States, only the largest release data about club activities for publication. In recent years, a number of banks have reported more than 100,000 Christmas Club accounts each, with annual distributions from these special savings plans exceeding $25,000,000 in large institutions. During one recent year, Connecticut's Deep River Savings Bank—one of the smallest reporting institutions—had 1,092 Christmas Club accounts, with participants saving an average of $197.15. In large urban areas average annual savings have reached or exceeded $500.

Some Washington insiders, who refuse to permit the use of their names, say that the potential long-range economic impact of the Christmas Club savings plan is far greater than it appears on the surface. According to them, the much-publicized tax-free personal savings plan so enthusiastically announced by President George Bush during his second year in office was inspired by, and is a direct descendant of, Merkel Landis's nickel-a-week Christmas Club.

Flower of the Blessed Night

"COME HERE, JUAN. SOMETHING STRANGE has happened."

"What is it, sir?"

"See that hillside? Yesterday it was dark. This morning it is nearly covered with red flowers. I've never seen anything like it."

"We in Mexico are accustomed to it, Mr. Poinsett. Most years, the Flower of the Blessed Night makes its appearance on an evening near the holidays. Sometimes it happens on Christmas Eve."

"When I last walked where the flowers are now so vivid," Mr. Poinsett replied, "it seemed to be covered with weeds. Some of them are eight feet tall."

"The plants you thought were weeds *are* the marvelous flowers, sir. They were given to the people of Mexico by a miracle long ago."

"Please tell me about the miracle, Juan."

"One Christmas Eve, when everyone was going to the cathedral to worship, a poor little girl was very sad. Everyone else took along a gift to leave at the altar for the Christ Child. She had nothing.

"So when she came near the cathedral, she decided not to go in. Instead, she knelt on the cobblestones and offered a prayer of contrition. She told the Christ Child how very much she wanted to leave a beautiful gift at the altar.

"'Alas,' she said, 'I am empty handed. I have nothing at all to give you, and that makes me ashamed to enter the cathedral and approach the altar.'"

"I think I can understand the child's point of view, even though I am not Catholic," interjected Joel R. Poinsett, the U.S. Minister to Mexico.

World traveler Joel R. Poinsett collected plant specimens everywhere he went.

"Oh, I really feel for the little girl," Juan said. "It must have been a dreadful experience for her. But the Christ Child felt for her, too.

"When she finished her prayer and wiped her eyes, she looked around. In a little park adjoining the cathedral, she saw something moving. It was a green plant, gradually emerging from the earth. As soon as it was about four feet high, it miraculously burst into bloom. Splendid red flowers such as no one had ever seen before covered the top of the plant.

President John Quincy Adams sent Poinsett to Mexico as the United States' first ambassador.

"Joyful at having witnessed a miracle, the child broke off a handful of the crimson blossoms and took them to the altar. There she put them down as her gift to the Christ Child.

"All this happened a very long time ago, you understand. Gradually the marvelous plants spread from the park where they first appeared. Soon they grew throughout the city, and then they moved into the countryside. They kept spreading until all Mexico is now full of them.

"These plants bloom at the Christmas season and provide such beauty that people cannot help but be filled with holiday joy."

"A charming legend," Poinsett replied, "unlike any that I have heard elsewhere. But the plant is unique. I must have a close look at it today, perhaps at the time of siesta."

During the sultry afternoon hour when most Mexicans were napping, the American who had been in Mexico City for only a few months went on what he called a "field jaunt." He studied one plant after another with the trained eye of a veteran agriculturist.

Back at the embassy, he reported his findings to the Mexican aide.

"Those beautiful red flowers aren't flowers at all, Juan. They are leaves that for some unaccountable reason turn crimson at this season. Not all of them turn red at the same time, and if you look at a plant closely you probably will find that some of the leaves near the top are white and others are pink."

"Maybe so, sir. But if that's the case, where are the flowers?"

"I examined several specimens carefully, and I'm positive that the flowers are those small clusters of yellow leaves right at the top, in the center. These are the reproductive organs of the plants. The crimson

During an anti-American demonstration, Poinsett's only protection was the American flag.

'leaves' are what an expert would call 'bracts.' Bracts, or petallike leaves, certainly are beautiful, but they have nothing to do with the plant's reproduction."

During his four years as the first U.S. ambassador to Mexico, Joel Poinsett became thoroughly familiar with the people, animals, and plants of the nation. He was so interested in the Flower of the Blessed Night that he sent a number of specimens to his South Carolina plantation, where workers reported that it was difficult, but not impossible, to cultivate the plant.

John C. Frémont, whom Poinsett sent on an expedition to explore the West, became the first Republican candidate for the presidency.

Mexican farmers generally liked the man who asked so many questions and sometimes offered surprising answers. However, British influence was strong in Mexico, and most officials had little use for the American. During one stormy period of anti-American demonstrations, a mob threatened to take over the embassy. Poinsett faced them, pointed to the American flag as his only protection, and persuaded them to disband.

Tension subsided only briefly before it mounted once again. When Poinsett's position as ambassador became impossible, his long-time personal friend, President Andrew Jackson, decided in 1829 to recall him to the United States. After having been in Mexico a little more than four years, he surrendered his credentials and took his formal leave on Christmas Day 1830.

"Many of my memories of Mexico are less than pleasant," he later said. "But I shall never forget my joy at first seeing the Flower of the Blessed Night."

With cuttings having been distributed to many flower growers and botanists, interest in the plant with crimson bracts was strong by 1835. That is when Philadelphia botanist R. Buist notified Poinsett, "The beautiful scarlet bracts on a plant four months from cutting reached fourteen inches in diameter!" A few months earlier he had informed the former diplomat that American scientists had decided to call the plant the poinsettia in his honor.

At the Smithsonian Institution and other centers of research, scientists discovered that coloration of the bracts is governed by exposure

The Smithsonian Institute, deeply indebted to the work of Joel Poinsett.

to light. In and around Mexico City, the natural movements of the earth and the sun are perfect for bringing the plant into glorious crimson at the Christmas season. Commercial growers achieve the same result by timing their use of artificial light.

Joel R. Poinsett did not live to discover all the secrets of the Christmas plant that has made his name a household word throughout the developed world. If he could saunter through shopping malls, business and professional offices, and churches, and peer into millions of homes made bright by poinsettias, no doubt he would rejoice at having been the one who put a new measure of nature's red into the holiday season.

A Letter from Santa

We are only ninety days from Christmas. Every year, a great many boys and girls write to Santa Claus, some asking for things they want and others asking questions of Old Santa.

The policy of the Post Office Department has been to put letters addressed to Santa Claus into the dead letter file. Of course, no one comes to claim them, and eventually they are destroyed.

It has occurred to me that even a small number of persons, spending an hour or two a week, can make reasonable replies to questions addressed to Santa. That is why I am asking you—along with other friends and business associates—to join me in forming an association whose aim will be to preserve children's faith in Santa Claus.

A favorable reply, indicating your willingness to take part in this noble enterprise, will be appreciated more than words can say.

—John D. Gluck

WHEN THIS LETTER WAS SENT TO AN ESTImated 120 men and women in New York City in 1914, nearly half of them responded positively. A few even marked out the notation "an hour or two a week" and substituted such notes as "an hour a day, if needed," "ten hours a week," and "no time limit."

Once the Santa Claus Association was formed, Gluck made arrangements with postal authorities for weekly pickup of "Santa Claus letters" during the period prior to Thanksgiving. After that holiday, he went to the post office daily until just before Christmas.

As members of the Santa Claus Association opened letters, they read them and prepared handwritten replies to those that included questions. Following the guidance of fellow New Yorker Thomas

Nast, members of the association used the return address: Santa Claus, North Pole. Although a few people questioned the wisdom of that practice, John Gluck was emphatic. "When a boy or girl sees that magic return address," he insisted, "the Manhattan cancellation will not be noticed."

In addition to preparing Santa Claus mail, members often sent inexpensive gifts to children who wrote that they would not get anything if Santa did not provide it.

Initially, word of the work done by the Santa Claus Association received little publicity. However, when a heart-warming story of their activity was circulated by wire services, newspapers throughout the nation published it for their readers.

According to lore, one of the readers was a postmaster. After he read what was being done in distant New York, this Indiana native called a town meeting. "We are the persons who ought to be providing Santa Claus mail," he urged after sharing the story of the program launched by John Gluck. "Of all places in America, this is the special one to which children should write."

Turning to a long-time resident, he gestured for her to stand. "Anna has promised me to remind you of how our community became unique. Go ahead, Anna. Many of the younger people here do not know the details."

Speaking with a pronounced accent, Anna was hesitant at first but soon became enthusiastic. "Ve had yust six or eight families here at first. It was in 1852, I think. Everybody depended on the general store for the things they needed. They didn't need much. But some-

Envelope now used by "Santa's Elves" in Santa Claus, Indiana

one said, 'Ve must have a name for our village. No one knows what to call it.'

"They all came together in our Salem Methodist Church. It was on Christmas Eve, and they decided to sing a few songs before starting to name their place—ours, now.

"I never found out why, but someone suggested 'Santa Fe.' It sounded good, and people were about ready to choose it when a trader got up and spoke. He told the people he was yust back from visiting trading posts up and down the Ohio and that one of them was located at Santa Fe.

"When the people learned that our state already had a Santa Fe, they didn't know what to do. No one had a good idea about a name.

"Yust then, there was a noise outside. It was the music of yingle bells, and one of the children stood up and called out, 'Santa Claus! Santa Claus!'"

"I've heard that story all my life, but I never was sure it was true, Anna," a housewife interjected.

"True! True!" the older woman responded. "I know, because I got it from my own grandmother who was there. Once the people heard the little girl, they all said she had named the town. That is how it became Santa Claus. That very night."

"Thank you, Anna!" responded the postmaster. "I know the story well, but I didn't get it from my grandmother. My own father told me that the federal government decided to put a post office here in 1856. At first, Washington didn't want to use Santa Claus, but when the old folks wrote letters and told about the meeting in the church, they decided to make this Santa Claus, Indiana.

"It really should not have been hard for them to reach that decision," Martin chuckled as he continued. "After all, we are only fourteen miles from Siberia and fifteen miles from Holland. Ireland and Algiers are not quite so close, but on the map they seem very near. Colorful names are all around us."

Turning to his motive for asking folk to come together, he pointed out, "We've been sitting here as Santa Claus for more than fifty years. In all that time nothing much has been done about it. I think we

Jim Yellig, who to friends and relatives was Santa Claus, answered stacks of letters.

ought to begin encouraging children to send their letters right here instead of to New York or some other place. And I will answer every one of them myself!"

Martin drew enthusiastic applause, and several of his listeners volunteered to help write to children. As news of the enterprise spread, the volume of mail grew so great that postmaster Martin had to ask for aid from members of the American Legion post.

Robert L. Ripley's famous "Believe It or Not" feature centered upon the village during the Christmas holidays of 1927. From that time forward, the volume of mail increased even more rapidly. In addition to children, adults began asking that their greeting cards be hand-stamped with the magic postmark.

By the end of the Great Depression, workers at the tiny post office were canceling one thousand stamps a day at the peak of the Christmas season. The volume of mail created a problem since it had to be hauled twelve miles to the nearest railroad.

In the nation's capital, officials decided to solve the problem by abolishing the Santa Claus post office. When this decision was made

Santa Claus (Jim Yellig) never revealed what Ronald Reagan wanted for Christmas.

public, the national protest was so strong that the ruling was rescinded.

The volume of letters written in response to youngsters who wrote Santa soon passed fifty thousand annually. Jim Yellig, who headed teams of volunteers that handled the letters for twenty-five years, admitted that he was sometimes harried.

"We have nearly one-third of the people of Santa Claus involved in answering letters now," he said a few years ago. "Other volunteers come from nearby towns to help during the rush season."

Born in 1894, Yellig spent twenty years in the U.S. Navy before returning home to Spencer County, Indiana. Soon he began to be Santa at Christmas, and then he assumed responsibility for handling mail addressed to the spirit of Christmas.

For years Yellig wore a splendid natural beard, snow white, of course. He shaved it off only when he found himself identified as Santa Claus even when "on vacation and wearing typical Florida clothes." He acquired four pairs of natty red velvet pants, and at age seventy-two explained, "The right leg always wears out first. That's the one most children prefer to sit on."

Seeing the need for a continuing organization to answer letters, Jim Yellig formed Santa's Elves. Initially he was aided by Mabel Ryan and postmaster Mary Ann Long. Today, Garden Club members and senior citizens reply to children, and Santa's Elves, headed by Jim's daughter Patricia (Mrs. William A. Koch), provide postage. The volume of mail to Santa Claus is not as great as it was when the cost of sending letters was low and Jolly Saint Nick was seen infrequently. Yet residents say the annual cascade of mail, becomes "tremendous" as Christmas approaches.

[Children may still write to Santa Claus at his Indiana home, and adults who wish information about having cards postmarked there may address inquiries with a self-addressed return envelope to: Postmaster, Santa Claus, IN 47579.]

The First Teddy Bear

"HEY, MORRIS. YOU'RE ALWAYS WANTING TO know what it means to be an American. Got something to show you."

"Looks like a newspaper, Ralph."

"That's what it is. One of the fellows at the plant has a brother who's on a construction job in Washington. He sent the *Evening Star* from last Thursday. Thought some of us New Yorkers might get a kick out of it."

"Let me see it then."

"Hold on a second. Back in Russia where you came from, you know who's in charge. But before I let you look at the cartoon, you've gotta tell me the name of the president of the United States."

Morris Michtom thought for a moment, formed his mouth to pronounce a name, and then looked at his wife. She nodded encouragement, so he said, "Rose-e-veldt."

"Right, old timer! You hit the target first crack out of the barrel! Here," Ralph Richie said while opening the folded newspaper with a flourish, "feast your eyes on *this*!"

"It's a man with great big glasses and a gun, and there's a little animal in front of him," Morris said, more to himself than to the American who had taken him under his wing.

"Not just a man! That's Teddy Roosevelt, president of the United States, and a fellow down in Washington is making fun of him in public! Clifford Berryman couldn't get away with that in Russia, could he, now?"

"No. And he doesn't know much about bears, either. Back in the Old Country, we have lots of them, and I never saw one that looks like this animal."

Armed with rifle and hunting knife, buckskin-clad Roosevelt posed without spectacles [HARVARD UNIVERSITY].

"It's a black bear, you Rushkie immigrant! You don't have 'em where you came from. And it's a female, see! That cartoon fellow has the president of the United States on a hunting trip, unable to flush out anything but a little ole female, and then he refuses to shoot her. Sorta makes a monkey out of the great bear hunter, don't you think?"

"Maybe," admitted Michtom. "But maybe it just shows that the head of the United States of America is a kind gentleman."

Theodore Roosevelt, outdoorsman and mighty hunter.

"No way. Newspapers don't print that sort of cartoons. This one makes fun of the man you call Rose-e-veldt. If a fellow tried to get away with that kind of joke back where you came from, he'd wind up in Siberia before the end of the week. Another lesson in democracy, pal!"

Ralph Richie continued, "Our president—he's yours now, too, remember—went on a hunting trip 'way down south, and it was big news when he didn't have any luck. You can read all about it in the *Times.*"

"Can't afford it. I don't have a penny a day to throw away."

"Then beat it down to the library and look through the papers for the last week or ten days. You'll find a lot about the hunting trip."

"After the busy season is over, maybe I will. But right now, since you went to all the trouble of bringing that Washington paper, how about just leaving it with me and the wife?" the Russian immigrant asked.

"Maybe. What in the world do you want with it?"

"This Rose-e-veldt is a very great man. People like to know about him and what he is doing. I think perhaps I will make a bear and put it in my window. It will catch the eyes of people, and some of them will come into my toy shop."

"Sounds good. Cut out the cartoon and paste it on your window. And be sure to fix a nice, big sign. Call your new toy 'Teddy's Bear.' That ought to bring you some business."

Poring over several November 1902 issues of the *New York Times,* Michtom told his wife, "Americans are very interested in their president. So much so that this big newspaper told a lot about that hunting trip in a place called Yazoo County, Mississippi.

"It all started with a railroad man named Fish. Why on earth would anybody have such a name as that? Anyway, Mr. Stuyvesant Fish owns a lot of land in the South, and he took the president down there to hunt a black bear. . . ."

Morris Michtom and his wife stayed up very late each evening of the third week of November 1902. Their neighbors wondered why the lights burned so long in their Brooklyn apartment. They discovered the reason when Teddy's Bear went on display in Morris's shop.

"What's the new toy worth?" a stranger demanded as Christmas drew near.

"She's not for sale," Mrs. Michtom responded. "My husband made only one of them. Besides, she has movable arms and legs and head. Come back maybe next year."

The long-loved Teddy Bear, still a popular toy with children.

Christmas was barely over before the toy maker and his wife began hand-sewing stuffed bears for the following season. Complete with button eyes, Teddy's Bear was an instant success.

"We gotta money enough to buy a fine house in Flatbush—thirty-five hundred, with two hundred down," Morris announced in mid-December.

"No, no! No house!" his wife protested. "Already the business is good, but it will be better. Use the money from Teddy's Bear to start up a real company."

Acting on his wife's insistence, Michtom consulted his American friend about a name and settled upon the Ideal Novelty and Toy Company. Years later, with the name abbreviated to Ideal Toy Company, it became widely respected as the world's largest toy manufacturer.

Ironically, had Roosevelt allowed more members of the press to accompany the hunting expedition for a black bear, the Teddy Bear might never have been created. Only three reporters—representatives of press associations—had been allowed in the hunting camp, and several reporters and photographers who tried to crash the camp were turned back by armed guards. It may have been resentment that

This photograph inspired a game, complete with a tiny tin Roosevelt, that was popular for a short time.

the *Washington Evening Star* had not been allowed to cover the hunt that aroused Clifford Berryman to turn Roosevelt's refusal to shoot a captured female bear into a mocking cartoon. Had he not done so, and had Morris Michtom's American friend not shown him the cartoon, the expedition would have been forgotten long ago.

Not so, however. Michtom changed the toy's name to Teddy Bear, and it has proved perennially popular. Originally handsewn for sale at about seventy-five cents, the Teddy Bear is now available every Christmas in a size and at a price to fit all tastes.

England's Prince Charles, who will be king one day, has his favorite Teddy Bear, which is battered and worn, but much loved. According to biographer Andrew Morton in *Diane's Diary,* at mid-life His Royal Highness has the little fellow safely stowed in his luggage whenever he travels abroad.

A Candy Cane for Everyone

"YOUR CANDY CANES ARE RICH IN SYMBOLISM. Why don't you make enough so everyone can have them during the Christmas season?"

"Harding, you're right about the symbolism. I wish every Christian in America could realize it. But I thought you knew that candy canes are made entirely by hand, with a lot of waste. I doubt they will ever be produced commercially at a profit."

"Why not?" mused Father Harding Keller, who already held two valuable patents. "Surely someone can invent a machine to eliminate most or all of the labor."

"You do it then, Harding," responded Bob McCormack. Head of a candy manufacturing company in Albany, Georgia, McCormack was extremely fond of his brother-in-law and looked forward to his annual visits from Arkansas. "Your sister tells me that you got started inventing things when you were a small boy."

Father Harding Keller [COURTESY BOBS CANDIES, Inc.].

"I guess she's right," admitted Father Keller. "But I remember one of my inventions also got me into hot water . . . sort of."

"You mean your hot water machine? I've heard about it, but tell me the real story."

"It was my first genuine invention," began Keller, who in 1949 was priest of a Catholic parish in North Little Rock, Arkansas. "When I was a small boy, the men in our family took turns cranking the wringer of the washing machine. It was the best thing on the market at the turn of the century, but my arms would get so tired. When I complained to my mother, she explained that leg muscles are stronger than arms.

"So I got busy and, with the help of my father and brother, rigged up a way to attach my bicycle to the old washing machine. That way we were able to use our leg muscles to crank the wringer."

The next day Father Keller put on his old gray pants and a work shirt and went to the candy plant. There he watched the stick candy makers at work, knowing that if he was successful at inventing a machine that would make candy canes, Christmas would never be the same.

A few candy canes, mostly for local use, had already been produced by McCormack's workers. They started by combining 300 pounds of sugar with 240 pounds of corn syrup and 50 pounds of water. Put into a huge kettle, this "premelt" was mixed with a large boat paddle and heated to 240 degrees to get all the water out of it. Then it was put into a continuous cooker, where it was heated another 48 degrees to produce a batch of candy "ropes" that were soft enough to be twisted by hand.

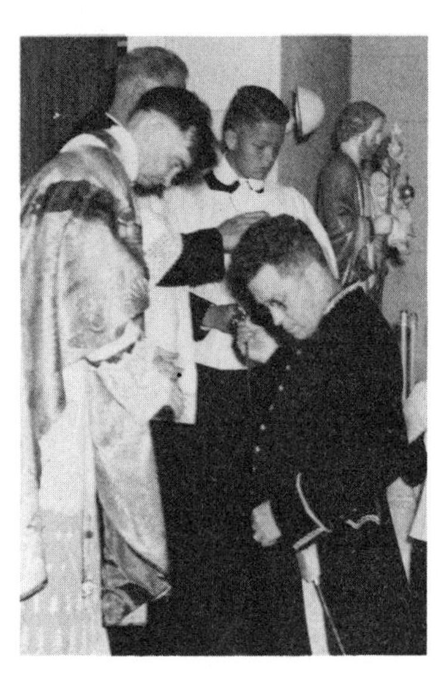

Mr. Bob McCormack during his investiture as a Knight of the Order of Saint Sylvester [COURTESY BOBS CANDIES, INC.].

Men standing at two ends of the table twisted the twenty-foot ropes so the stripes would spiral around the candy. Then, after a stick was cut, the crook was added by hand to make a cane. It was an involved, expensive, and wasteful process.

Six months later, Father Keller had invented his candy cane machine. As McCormack was delighted to see when Keller had assembled and tested it in Albany, it actually produced candy sticks of uniform thickness, already twisted.

There was one flaw, however. Once the patented "Keller machine" moved into full speed, it scattered candy all over the room. "I fixed that problem by added cups that counteracted the centrifugal force of the machine," the priest-inventor later explained. "Once those cups were added, my machine would twist and cut 160 sticks a minute, with very little waste. The wooden molds I used also meant that the sticks could be made into canes while still warm."

Soon Father Keller developed another machine for bending the crooks. Finally hand labor had been eliminated from the manufacturing process.

By 1959 Bobs was recognized as the world's largest producer of candy canes. Earlier, it had taken three men a full hour to cut and twist one hundred pounds of candy. With the Keller machine and the bending device, one man could twist and cut six hundred pounds an hour. Production of candy canes soon soared to a previously unthinkable level of a half-million canes per eight-hour shift.

Bob McCormack, a devout churchman, launched an intensive search for the history and symbolism of the candy cane. "It is a logical piece to have around the house at Christmas," he insisted, "because it reminds us of the crooks carried by the shepherds who figure so prominently in the biblical Christmas story."

Soon after Europeans adopted the use of Christmas trees, they began making special decorations for them. Food items predominated, with cookies and candy heavily represented. That is when straight, white sticks of sugar candy came into use at Christmas, probably during the seventeenth century.

Tradition has it that some of these candies were put to use in Cologne Cathedral about 1670 while restless youngsters were attending ceremonies around the living crèche. To keep them quiet, the choirmaster persuaded craftsmen to make sticks of candy bent at the end to represent shepherds' crooks, then he passed them out to boys and girls

An advertisement for Bobs Candies' first packages of candy canes made automatically and packaged for shipment [COURTESY BOBS CANDIES, INC.].

who came to the cathedral. From Cologne, the custom of handing out "souvenir" sugar crooks at living crèche ceremonies spread throughout Europe. Soon the white canes were embellished with sugar roses.

About 1847, August Imgard of Ohio managed to decorate his Christmas tree with candy canes to entertain his nephews and nieces. Many who saw his canes went home to boil sugar and experiment with canes of their own.

It took nearly another half century before someone added stripes to the canes, although neither Bob McCormack nor Father Keller ever learned the inventor's name. They did, however, find that Christmas cards produced before 1900 show plain white canes, while striped ones appear on many cards printed early in the twentieth century.

Today's candy cane includes two large stripes and two sets of smaller stripes that spiral around the stick. "The candy cane's white background symbolizes purity," Father Keller often told people. "Red, which is the color of blood, reminds us of sacrifice. The wide red stripe on a cane symbolizes the sacrifice of Christ, while the smaller red ones stand for the sacrifices that must be made by His followers."

Early striped canes were sometimes flavored with wintergreen, but peppermint soon became standard. According to McCormack family research, even the peppermint flavor is appropriate since it is akin to the biblical herb hyssop, which represents healing.

Today's peppermint-flavored, striped candy cane is a visual reminder of the shepherd's staff and a focal point for meditation upon purity and sacrifice.

McCormack's son, daughter, grandson, and other close relatives are now involved in Bobs Candies, Inc. Contact with these devout believers leaves an observer convinced that they are doing more than simply making good candy for shipment throughout the world. They believe, and hope, that occasionally a red-striped candy cane may prod someone to find the faith centered in the Babe whose first visitors carried crooks upon their shoulders.

Part Five

Resounding Deeds That Echo Still

Joy and celebration are central to Christmas, but they do not begin to exhaust its meaning. Over and over, persons playing leading roles on the world stage have taken decisive actions during the holy season.

Individual rights and liberty, as known in the English-speaking world, gained legal status at Christmas in A.D. 1214. Centuries later, it was during the holiday season that a crusader took steps that led to the abolition of slavery in Britain.

Not all transforming events are political, legal, or military, however. If you are reading by artificial light, the chances are very good that you are more greatly indebted to Christmas events than you know!

The Birth of Liberty

IN NOVEMBER 1214, A GROUP OF ENGLISH BARONS made a "pious" pilgrimage to an abbey northeast of London, but in fact they did little praying and a great deal of talking about their complaints against their king, John.

"Christmas is the time to force his hand," a northern baron suggested.

"Why then?" countered a southern baron. "He thinks no more of the birth of Christ than he does of a litter of hounds."

"We all know he was born on Christmas Eve," the former responded, "and he customarily celebrates the season with pomp and merriment. Heretofore none of us has dared decline a royal summons to join him. But this year let no man go to Worcester Castle. We'll set him off balance and thus have the upper hand in parley."

The barons then agreed to take a secret oath to unite, as John's old enemy, the archbishop of Canterbury, Stephen Langton, had suggested they do. Their plan worked, and a furious King John—alone at Christmas except for his retainers—agreed to a meeting with his vassals. It took place at London's New Temple on Twelfth Night (January 6), 1215, at the climax of the Christmas season.

King John, as depicted in a medieval document.

The fourth and youngest son of Henry II and Eleanor of Aquitaine, John had become king after the death of his brother Richard, known to history as a man with the "heart of a lion." Although John is often regarded as one of England's worst and most unpopular kings, a ruthless and cruel Machiavellian, the English-speaking world owes far more to the vices of John than to the labors of more virtuous sovereigns.

His reign began badly. He was suspected of the murder of his nephew, whom many considered the rightful heir to the throne.

Then he had the misfortune to face three formidable adversaries.

First, the French king succeeded in wresting from him vast lands England claimed in France, including the powerful dukedom of Normandy. Then, because of a bitter dispute with the pope, he was excommunicated from the church and England was placed under *interdict,* meaning all church services were banned.

Finally, he met resistance in the English barons. His quarrel with them arose from his ruthlessness in raising money for the campaign in France and from his practice of severely punishing vassals without a trial. When he had won absolution by the pope, he had sworn to Stephen Langton, archbishop of Canterbury, that he would "restore the good laws of his predecessors," but John violated his oath.

It was upon his return to England after the crushing defeat at Bouvines by the French, that the hostile barons renounced their homage and drew up their list of demands. They began lengthy negotiations on January 6 and on June 15, 1215, in a meadow called Runnymede on the banks of the Thames near London, forced him to sign a historic document.

Magna Carta (Great Charter) was described by Winston Churchill as "the most famous milestone of our rights and freedom," and its ideals eventually were incorporated into the U.S. Constitution.

Freedom of the church from royal interference and some guarantee of rights for the rising middle class in the towns were given. However, members of the lowest classes, the largest in the kingdom, were dealt with only in passing.

Magna Carta was a feudal, special-interest document, and its influence comes from the fact that as time passed some of its provisions took on new and expanded meanings.

For example, one article stated: "No scutage or aid, save the customary feudal ones, shall be levied, except by the common consent of the realm." In 1215 this simply meant that John would have to consult his "great council" of barons and bishops before levying special feudal dues. The provision later grew into the concept that taxation without representation is tyranny, an idea that would have amazed those at Runnymede.

King John signing the Magna Carta, as depicted by a modern artist.

Similarly, the provision that "No freeman shall be arrested or imprisoned, or dispossessed or outlawed or banished or in any way molested . . . unless by the lawful judgment of his peers and by the law of the land" meant that the barons wished to be tried only by their social equals, and they were putting in check abuses of royal justice. Eventually these points were enlarged into the rights of due process and trial by a jury of one's "peers."

Medieval kings of England reissued the charter with some changes about forty times, although the Tudors ignored it. However, it became an important precedent in the revolt against the Stuarts in the seventeenth century. At that time the rebels against the "divine right of kings" read into the medieval articles many of the same meanings that twentieth-century people see at once.

Therefore the enduring importance of Magna Carta lies in how it was later interpreted and in two principles that underlie the whole document: the king is subject to the law and may be required to abide by it.

For these reasons Magna Carta, whose preparation began at the Christmas season 1214, is still of utmost importance today.

"We Will End This Abomination"

"IS THIS THE *KING'S OWN*, AND ARE YOU BOUND for the Indies?"

"What's it to you, mister?"

"I hold a writ of *habeas corpus* that requires the release of the slave Sommersett. Is he aboard?"

"Maybe so, maybe not. It's none of my affair. I'm here to watch the ship. You Londoners don't seem to be able to stay away from us."

"I am on business of the court. Out of my way, fellow!"

The burly sailor surveyed diminutive Granville Sharp, age thirty-six, and retorted, "Why don't you try giving me a shove, mister?"

"That won't be necessary. Look! Here's the official order. I can have you locked up, if you prefer to spend a night or two in gaol. Show me below at once, or I will call the nearest constable."

Grumbling, the sailor stepped aside and muttered, "Go ahead, but find your own way around."

In the hold of the vessel moored in the Thames River, Sharp, who had never been to sea, stumbled around until his eyes became accustomed to the dim light. He then discovered a black male, manacled and lying on straw while trying to keep his feet out of the bilge water.

"Are you James Sommersett?"

"Yes, sir."

"Then on your feet, man. I have come to release you!"

"Don't know what you mean, sir."

"My name is Granville Sharp, and I have secured an order that forbids the master of this ship to move you toward Jamaica until you have appeared in court. Wait here. I will call a constable and see that your manacles are removed at once."

With Sommersett in tow, self-taught attorney Sharp made his way to his bachelor lodgings and turned once more to his legal books to prepare the argument he planned to make on the following day.

William Murray, first earl of Mansfield and former speaker of the House of Lords, was brusque. With the Christmas season already in progress, he was annoyed at having been delegated to hear another plea, especially from Sharp, who was regarded as a nuisance by many Londoners.

"We cannot simultaneously honor the birth of the Christ Child and hold men and women in bondage. . . ."
—Granville Sharp

Although he was a grandson of an archbishop of York, Granville Sharp did not fit smoothly into the society of his day. When hardly out of his teens, he began to agitate for parliamentary reform, then turned his attention to Ireland, demanding that it be given its independence.

"What on earth makes a grammar school graduate who spent years as apprentice to a Quaker linen draper so persistent in his work for the underdog?" an exasperated official demanded one day. Trying to answer his own question, he mused, "Must get some kind of satisfaction out of it. But for the life of me, I don't know how. He's a bloody Don Quixote who never spent a day in Spain. That's what he is!"

That assessment was strengthened in 1774 when Sharp published on behalf of the American colonists *A Declaration of the People's Natural Right to a Share in the Legislature.* Two years later, in a futile bid to dramatize his support for Americans whom his nation branded as rebels, Sharp resigned from his position in the Ordnance Department.

Everyone who had dealings with the self-appointed crusader regarded him as stubborn, impossibly idealistic, and just a hair this side of insane. He spent his days working to pay for bed and bread and his nights in study so he would be better prepared for his next appearance before a magistrate or judge.

To Chief Justice Mansfield, reluctantly sitting on the bench instead of helping to give his manor its final decorative touches for the holidays, the plaintiff was a nuisance. Drumming with his fingers, he listened to Sharp explain the issue. James Sommersett, a slave pur-

English traders and seamen handled more than half of all the slaves annually sent to the New World [LIBRARY OF CONGRESS].

chased in Virginia, had been brought to England by James Stewart. Once in the new land, he refused to continue to serve his master. Stewart was enraged; so he had the slave arrested and put aboard a ship bound for the New World, where he was to be sold.

"This story has been told a thousand times," Justice Mansfield snapped. "What, if anything, is new in the case I am asked to hear?"

"Since every Englishman cherishes his freedom, rooted in our own Magna Carta, there is no place on this free island for a slave, your honor. It is my contention that the moment a slave sets foot on English soil, he instantly and automatically becomes free!"

"That is not the ruling handed down in 1729," snapped Mansfield. "It was decided that neither residence in England nor baptism affects a master's right and property in a slave."

"I know, your honor. I also know that Blackstone himself has said that the ruling must stand. He told me that, himself, a few years ago. I know that owners regularly offer rewards for runaways. I know that auctions are advertised in our London newspapers. But I also know that these things are not right and never will be. They are contrary to the heart and soul of the common law that is the foundation of this great land of ours!

"Perhaps it is the work of Providence that the matter of James Sommersett has come up at this time. Surely you cannot, sir, close your eyes to the fact that we cannot simultaneously honor the birth of the Christ Child and hold men and women in bondage on this free island. I not only seek a declaration that this man became free the moment he took his first step here, I expect to prosecute James Stewart for having unlawfully detained James Sommersett aboard ship."

Mansfield shook his head in dismay, troubled by the argument. After meditating, he ruled that the case brought before him at Christmas 1771 must be referred to the full court.

Later, speaking for the court, Lord Mansfield rendered a clear-cut decision. In spite of long-established custom and regardless of the huge economic losses that owners must suffer, Granville Sharp was

Many wealthy Londoners used slaves as coachmen for their fancy carriages.

Especially on festive days, boats filled the Thames River at London [JOHN GRIFFIER PAINTING].

right. "Whatever inconveniences may follow from this decision," the judge reported, "I cannot say that this case is either allowed or approved by the law of England. Therefore, the black must be discharged."

"Slavery," continued the legal opinion, "is so odious that nothing can be suffered to support it but positive law [which did not appear in statute books]. The air of England has long been too pure for a slave, and every man is free who breathes it. Every man who comes here is entitled to the protection of English law, whatever oppression he may have suffered and whatever may be the colour of his skin."

Issued as the verdict of the full court, the famous Mansfield decision meant that slavery ceased to exist in the British Isles. It was the first giant step toward abolishing slavery in the Western world.

Granville's Sharp's victory was tempered with irony. At the time he secured a writ of *habeas corpus* for James Sommersett, British ships were carrying to the New World more than half of all slaves transported there each year.

Fresh Hope for Patriots

"YOU ARE UNUSUALLY SILENT THIS MORNING, General."

"There is little to talk about."

"Are you still fretting over the loss of General Lee?"

"God forbid! I am simply thankful that 2,700 or so of his men managed to cross the Delaware and escape. I do not pretend to understand Major General Charles Lee. He was sleeping in a house guarded by only two sentries when the British discovered him. No man in his senses would take such a chance."

American General Charles Lee was captured by men of the British Sixteenth Dragoons [THE PARKER GALLERY].

"I am sure you are right, General. But it is the talk of the camp that you have made up your mind to take a great chance, and soon."

"Perhaps. You will know immediately, once I have made up my mind, Colonel Fitzgerald. Until then, remember that the days ahead may offer us our last opportunity to infuse new lifeblood into our sadly battered cause."

"You're talking about the enlistment issue, General Washington?"

"Of course. At the stroke of midnight on the thirty-first, we stand to lose at least one-fourth of our men, perhaps as many as one-third. Do you know where that will leave the Continental army?"

"Afraid so, General. You will be in command of no more than 1,500 men, and maybe a few units of the Massachusetts militia if they respond to your plea for help."

"If news gets out that the commander-in-chief heads only a handful of veterans," Washington confided, "I fear that the hopes of our countrymen will be dashed. Many are despondent already, you know."

"Because they are hungry for a British defeat, you mean?"

"Of course. Since I took command in Philadelphia eighteen months ago, we have not had a significant victory. Many brave Amer-

General Sir Henry Clinton, supreme commander of British forces in North America [THOMAS DAY MINIATURE].

icans have lost heart. That accounts for the Jerseymen who accepted pardons from the king and have sworn new loyalty to him."

"Then everything, or practically everything, is lost?"

"Certainly not, Colonel. But we have little time . . . so little time. But enough of such sentiments. I have important letters to write, even though it is Christmas Eve."

Turning his back upon Col. John Fitzgerald, George Washington strode to his headquarters tent. Writing with great speed, he sent Col. Samuel Griffin detailed instructions about a new method of forming recruits into companies.

A long, urgent letter to the Continental Congress detailed his plight. Following that, he dispatched messages to Passamaquoddy Indian chieftains and to the Indians of the St. John's River area. Hoping to have his tattered army strengthened by Indian allies, he warned, "Now, brothers, never let the King's wicked counsellors turn your hearts against me and your brethren of this country."

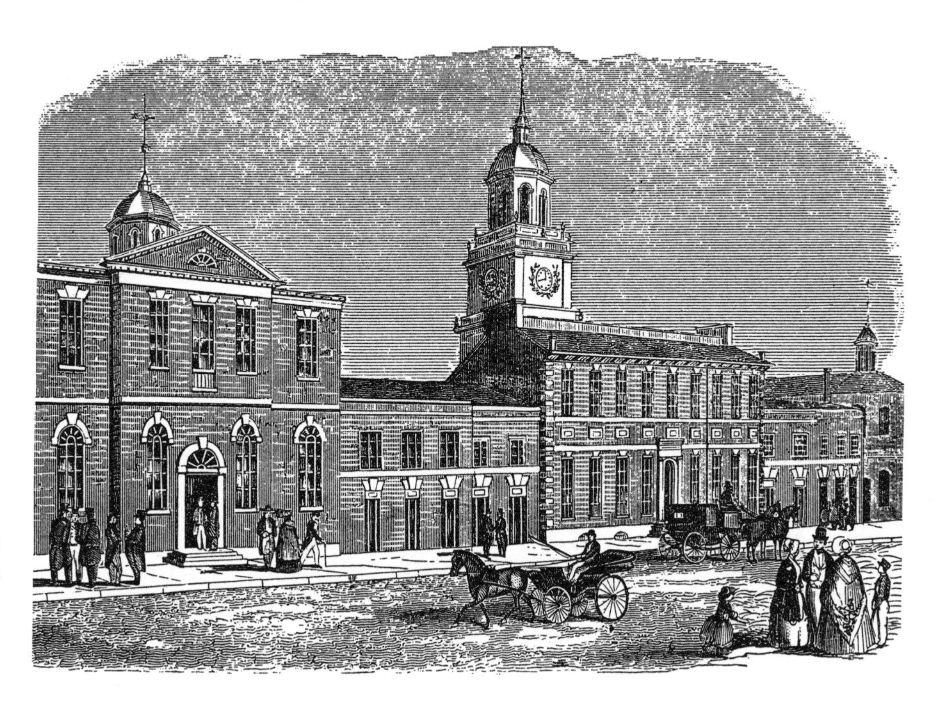

The State House, Philadelphia, was long the center of colonial lawmaking.

Two more letters, one to Robert Morris and the other to Gen. Israel Putnam, warned of a likely British attack on Philadelphia.

Washington's most important Christmas Eve message was not written, however, but was delivered orally to his top aides. Confirming the rumor which Fitzgerald had mentioned, he gave terse orders to advance upon the town of Trenton, New Jersey.

"We will cross the Delaware River late on Christmas Day in Durham boats, using darkness as cover," he said. "Advancing on foot from the river to the town, we will strike an hour before dawn on the twenty-sixth. It is a desperate undertaking, to be sure. But it is our last great hope. Gentlemen, you and your men must not fail me in this crucial hour!"

Hungry men wearing the ragged remnants of blue-and-buff uniforms grumbled and cursed at being ordered into combat six days before their enlistments expired. They moved forward as directed, however, even though those whose shoes were worn out or missing left bloody footprints in the snow as they headed toward the river.

Ice on the Delaware, no more than a skin at noon on Christmas Day, had hardened to a shell overnight. An hour of rain softened the ice, but when the skies cleared a wave of cold air made it harder than before. Fed by melting snow, the river was at flood stage, moving so rapidly that huge, jagged sheets of ice rotated as they floated downstream, making it almost impassable.

British commander Lord Howe, who used German mercenaries to bolster the strength of his army.

After gazing at the angry river for a while, George Washington ordered a company of engineers to cut additional poles for propelling the clumsy boats. Three hours after midnight, with the ice becoming heavier and only 2,400 men across the river, Washington signaled to bring the crossing to a halt. Waving his sword toward Trenton, nine miles away, he shouted, "Victory, or death!"

In the predawn hours of December 26, scouts spotted moving silhouettes ahead. Spurring his horse into a gallop, Washington confronted the strangers.

"Sir, we are a company of Virginians," their captain explained. "Yesterday we were dispatched across the Delaware to scout the land. Somehow, we stumbled into Trenton. When a sentry ran out, we fired several rounds and beat a hasty retreat."

"Washington at the Passage of the Delaware," as depicted by Thomas Sully [MUSEUM OF FINE ARTS, BOSTON, MASSACHUSETTS].

Thinking only briefly, Washington realized that the Hessians quartered in Trenton would be on their guard. It was too late to turn back, so—wordless—he waved his sword to order his men forward.

In a tiny settlement that the Hessians were using as an outpost, a German sentry saw the ice-covered Americans approaching. *"Der Feind! Heraus! Heraus!"* ("The enemy! To your feet! To your feet!") he cried.

His warning was useless. Using the hit-and-run tactics he had learned from Indians, Washington directed his Continentals as they swarmed the outpost and took the sentries as prisoners. Then he divided his troops into several columns to hit Trenton from all sides.

At Trenton the converging Continental forces met sleepy Hessian troops just roused from bed. Resistance was slight, and in less than forty minutes the town was in Continental hands. Casualties were surprisingly light. Washington's regiments suffered only five and the Hessians counted just thirty.

The impact of Washington's victory at Trenton was far greater than its military significance.

"Nine hundred Hessians captured!" gloated John Adams, who earlier had found himself jealous when Washington was given the military post he wanted. "Our brave Continentals seized six splendid German brass cannon, along with wagonloads of arms and supplies!"

In Philadelphia Robert Morris rejoiced that as a result of Washington's stunning victory. "Continental currency is being accepted somewhat more readily, while farmers and merchants have begun to release their hoarded goods to commissary officers."

Lord Howe, the British commander, ordered his men to give up the remainder of their most advanced posts, leaving New Jersey virtually free of Redcoats. This sudden turn of events affected many citizens who had called themselves Loyalists to escape British harassment. With the colony no longer under British domination, large numbers of one-time Loyalists suddenly became patriots.

Robert Morris, financier of the American Revolution

Although "Washington Crossing the Delaware" depicts the incident as occurring in full light, the inaccurate version is highly popular.

* * *

On December 30, George Washington sat down to write a brief but very important memorandum: "I have the pleasure to acquaint you [members of the Continental Congress] that the Continental Regiments from the Eastern Government have, to a man, agreed to stay six weeks beyond their term of enlistment."

With his army intact and news of victory surging through the colonies, patriots who had been nearly ready to give up the struggle made new commitment to the cause. Everywhere, men and women declared, "We will support our leaders to the very end, come what may! Sooner or later, our little colonies will be free from British tyranny!"

A Struggle for Religious Freedom

James Madison

"THANK YOU FOR COMING, GENTLEMEN. I count each of you as a close friend, else I would not have asked you to participate in this conference so close to the holiday season."

"Glad to be here, Mr. Madison. You need our help with legislation, I assume."

"Yes. And it is of a particularly delicate nature. I hope that none of our discussion will leave this room."

James Madison pulled a sheaf of documents from his desk, sipped from his glass, and said he thought it was appropriate that he review pertinent events.

"Most or all of you gentlemen will remember that in 1779, Mr. Jefferson proposed to lawmakers a Bill for Establishing Religious Freedom."

"Of course we remember!" a colleague blurted. "I believe Jefferson was seldom, if ever, so badly defeated in the House."

"He was too far ahead of public opinion," Madison admitted.

"Humiliating to him as it was, his defeat was far from total. It was his bill, never enacted, that prompted the abolition of salaries for clergy of the established church. That was a first step toward my long-cherished goal of complete separation of church and state. But all of us know that in the Old Dominion it is still legally impossible to be married unless by an Anglican priest. Also, a Virginian who admits to holding heretical views is still subject to arrest and prosecution as a common criminal. It is a sad state of affairs, and I believe that now is the time to remedy it."

"Right now? As we approach the high holy day that marks the birth of Jesus Christ?"

"Right now!" tradition holds that Madison firmly responded.

According to orally transmitted lore, the defeat of Gov. Patrick Henry's campaign to re-establish the Episcopal Church meant that it was time to try again to seek full freedom of religion. Madison's passionate devotion to this cause was well known throughout the state.

Henry was universally hailed as Virginia's most persuasive speaker. Had he held a seat in the House of Delegates, declared Spencer Roane, "He could have demolished Madison with as much ease as Samson snapped the cords that bound him before he was shorn." However, having been elected in 1784 to his fourth term as governor, Henry was barred from debate on proposed legislation.

Thomas Jefferson's bill to foster religious freedom was defeated initially.

Although his tongue was temporarily muzzled, Patrick Henry's pen remained free, and he now proposed to infringe upon the liberty of his fellow citizens. Possibly influenced by the owners of the great Tidewater plantations, he proposed to levy a new tax "for the support of the Christian religion or of some other Christian church, denomination, or communion of Christians, or of some form of Christian worship."

Although cautiously worded, the resolution deceived few Virginians. Therefore, opposition persuaded Henry to modify the language of the proposal, even though it was endorsed by every Episcopal priest in the state. Accordingly, his new general assessment would be imposed "to provide support for teachers of the Christian religion."

At his Montpellier (now spelled Montpelier) home, James Madison branded the revision as having no effect, except perhaps to fool the credulous. After many days of intensive work, in June 1785 he produced an unsigned document that he had printed and circulated throughout the state.

Although it was anonymous, the "Memorandum and Remonstrance against Religious Assessments" was soon recognized to have come from Madison. "The Religion of every man must be left to the conviction and conscience of every man; and it is the right of every man to exercise it as these may dictate," Section 1 began. "It is the duty of every man to render to the Creator such homage and such only as he believes to be acceptable to him."

Warning that there is always danger that "the majority may trespass on the rights of the minority," Madison then proceeded: "Who does not see that the same authority which can establish Christianity, in exclusion of all other Religions, may establish with the same ease any particular sect of Christians, in exclusion of all other Sects? that the same authority which can force a citizen to contribute three pence only of his property for the support of any one establishment, may force him to conform to any other establishment in all cases whatsoever?"

Madison's arguments against the governor's resolution warned: "Whilst we assert for ourselves a freedom to embrace, to profess and to observe the Religion which we believe to be of divine origin [Christianity], we cannot deny an equal freedom to those whose minds have not yet yielded to the evidence which has convinced us. If this freedom be abused, it is an offence against God, not against man: To God, therefore, not to man, must an account of it be rendered."

Circulated throughout Virginia prior to the convening of the House of Delegates, it influenced public opinion to such a degree that it could not be ignored. Patrick Henry's aides persuaded him to let his proposal for a new church tax die without being brought to the floor for a vote.

In the aftermath of the sudden surrender, Madison called a number of conferences. According to him, the climate was conducive for resubmitting Thomas Jefferson's Act for Religious Freedom.

Careful shepherding of the Jefferson bill brought it to the floor of the House of Delegates on Christmas Eve 1784. Strong language in

Princeton College, where James Madison was educated.

the document caused a few delegates to leave the floor, convinced that they could not defeat the bill and unwilling to hear it once more.

Jefferson began by stating his convictions "that Almighty God hath created the mind free; that all attempts to influence it by temporal punishments or burthens, or by civil incapacitations [a reference to the requirement that a holder of public office be a Christian], tend only to beget habits of hypocrisy and meanness, and are a departure from the plan of the Holy Author of our religion."

Governor Patrick Henry strongly favored tax support of Christian (Episcopalian) churches.

Considered heretical by some churchmen, the act blasted "the impious presumption of legislators and rulers civil, as well as ecclesiastical who, being themselves but fallible and uninspired men, have assumed dominion over the faith of others." Such persons "set up their own opinions and modes of thinking as the only true and infallible [ones]," then try to impose them on others.

In what may have been his most powerful blast, the author of the Declaration of Independence denounced all devices aimed at requiring anyone "to furnish contributions of money for the propagation of opinions which he disbelieves." Such action by the state, said Jefferson, "is sinful and tyrannical."

Even these brief excerpts help to reveal why the Act for Establishing Religious Freedom had been defeated when it was first introduced. Once the legislation was enacted, however, Virginia—and the United States—was on the road toward complete separation of church and state and the freedom of religion that is basic to the Bill of Rights.

Thirty-five years after his legislative triumph, James Madison looked back over his career. Even considering the years he spent in the White House, he regarded his accomplishments on Christmas Eve in Williamsburg as among his most notable.

Writing in 1819 he said, "It was the universal opinion of the Century preceding the last that Civil Government could not stand without the prop of a Religious establishment, and that the Christian religion itself would perish if not supported by a legal provision for its Clergy. The experience of Virginia conspicuously corroborates the disproof of both opinions."

"Eighth Wonder of the World"

"BAD NEWS, MR. EDISON. YOUR FRIEND MARshall Fox has embarrassed us terribly. It could be the end of our enterprise."

"What on earth do you mean, Francis?" demanded the weary inventor.

"Have you seen the *New York Herald* for the twenty-first?" his aide responded.

"You know perfectly well that I have no time to read newspapers or anything else. Surely Fox has not violated our agreement! He couldn't possibly have misunderstood how important it is not to let the public know how far along we are."

"Well, he has," Francis Jehl responded soberly. "He or his editor has ignored your restrictions."

He then showed Thomas Edison the newspaper headlines:

EDISON'S LIGHT
THE GREAT INVENTOR'S TRIUMPH
IN ELECTRICAL ILLUMINATION

A SCRAP OF PAPER

IT MAKES A LIGHT WITHOUT GAS
OR FLAME, CHEAPER THAN OIL

SUCCESS IN A COTTON THREAD

Edison's aide continued, "He seems to have gotten his facts right, but the timing could not be worse. Doubters will want to see for themselves, and if we can't satisfy your investors, they may pull out."

Thomas Alva Edison, photographed in 1892

"Inform every man that we will work around the clock until we are ready to show the world," Edison responded.

"We can't do that now. It is just two days until Christmas."

"That means we must strike Christmas from the calendar. No man will be paid who does not follow my orders. Let me think a minute."

After making hasty mental calculations, the inventor announced, "We will invite the public on the last day of the year. That will be a fitting way to end 1879 and enter 1880."

"But, Mr. Edison, that means we must manufacture lamps, string wires, and handle a multitude of details during the holiday season. I don't think it can be done."

"Stop thinking then, Francis, and start notifying the staff. What better way to spend the Christmas season than by making ready to show the world a new source of light?"

Wearing a crumpled felt hat and a half-buttoned vest, with a white silk handkerchief around his throat, Thomas Edison worked twenty

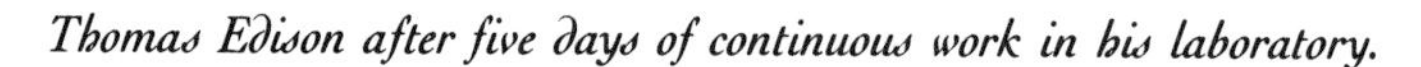

Thomas Edison after five days of continuous work in his laboratory.

hours out of every twenty-four. He dogged his staff of sixty to do the same thing.

"A few minutes of sleep will do you as much good as an hour," he said repeatedly. "And you don't need a bed or a cot. When I was a newsboy—twelve years old—I learned to nap on a wooden bench."

Edison's employees, who had heard that statement many times in earlier periods of crisis, grumbled behind his back. A few dared to protest, "This is no way to spend Christmas." There is no record, however, that any of his workers walked off the job.

On Christmas Eve there was a brief period of relaxation. Although he was deaf from a boyhood accident and lacked musical training, the inventor went to an organ where he managed to produce a few chords. Charles Batchelor whispered instructions to fellow workers while Edison played, then went to the keyboard. At his signal, the men gathered around the instrument for a clumsy but hearty rendition of a tribute to Edison, a parody of lines from Gilbert and Sullivan's *H. M. S. Pinafore:*

I am the Wizard of electric light,
And a wide-awake Wizard, too!

Platinum lead-in wires and carbonized sewing thread in high vacuum yielded a long-burn filament lamp.

Eager hordes of visitors began pouring into Menlo Park, New Jersey, on December 26, long before Edison was ready to demonstrate his invention.

Although newspaper stories informed readers that "the Edison light" would not be shown until the announced time, many felt they could not wait. So many people bought tickets for the journey to the tiny Menlo Park depot that on December 27 the Pennsylvania Railroad put on special trains to accommodate the traffic.

On the last night of the year, more than three thousand people swarmed through village streets to Edison's laboratory. There they found eight electric bulbs shining from wooden poles set up outside, two more above the entrance to the laboratory-library building, and thirty more inside the laboratory. One writer commented that the bulbs "made the place seem to be lighted by the midday sun!"

To newspaper reporters, Thomas Edison almost casually explained that he would illuminate all of Menlo Park with eight hundred lights. Then he would move on to Newark and then New York City. "My lamp will sell for twenty-five cents," he promised, "and it will cost only a few cents a day to operate."

No one present knew that it had taken two men six hours to pump the high vacuum required to manufacture a single bulb. Only a few dozen had been made.

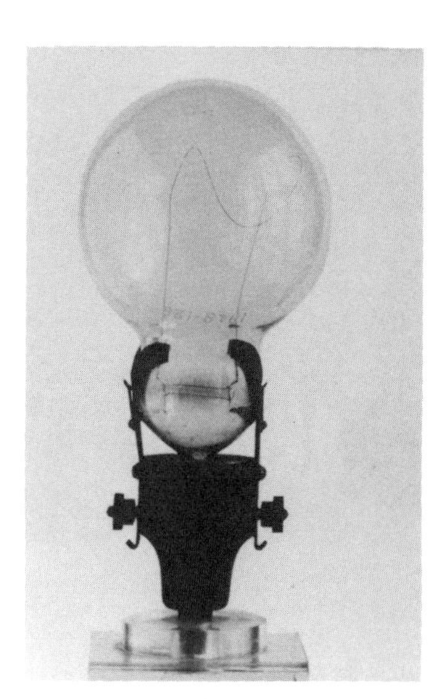

Edison's successful "filament lamp" used carbonized sewing thread.

Interestingly, an electrician then working for a Baltimore gas company produced some unexpected excitement. He edged into the laboratory with "a length of No. 10 wire around his sleeve and back, so that his hands would conceal the ends, and no one would know he had it."

His idea was to short-circuit Edison's creation, causing it to malfunction. He would then report how easily the electric light went out, and, presumably, investors would not abandon the stock of gas companies.

Edison, however, had anticipated the possibility of industrial sabotage and had installed a fuse. When the visitor made his attempt, only four lamps went out.

Glowing newspaper accounts of Edison's Christmas demonstration caused stock of the Edison Electric Light Company to jump in value by 600 percent—to $3,500. J. Pierpont Morgan and other financial backers more than doubled their commitment by advancing an additional $57,568 to Edison, enough capital to make it possible for him to begin plans for a separate building in which to manufacture the lamps and to talk of creating "a giant factory in Schenectady, before long."

Neither astonished newspaper readers who read of the "Eighth Wonder of the World" nor Wall Street financiers whose faith in Edison made it possible were aware that because of unwanted publicity he had recklessly demonstrated an invention not yet patented. On January 27, 1880—nearly a month after it was demonstrated to the general public and rival inventors—Edison's electric bulb was granted U.S. patent number 233,898.

Part Six

Christmas at the White House

As it is observed today, Christmas was late in reaching the White House. The earliest chief executives and their wives had few of the amenities and followed hardly any of the customs that now prevail. Because the White House is in many respects the pulse-point of the nation, holiday observances by First Families have been affected by the personalities of presidents and national and international events.

The First Family Celebrates

BECAUSE THE YOUNG AMERICAN GOVERNMENT was first situated in New York and then Philadelphia, George and Martha Washington never lived in the White House. It was in Philadelphia, the City of Brotherly Love, that they first invited guests to call at Christmas. There Lady Washington, as Martha was known at the time, presided over the "levee," a title long applied to all presidential receptions.

George Washington made it a rule never to shake hands with those who attended one of his Christmas levees.

Dressed to receive the holiday guests, the Father of His Country had his hair generously powdered, then donned a velvet coat and velvet breeches, as well as silver knee and shoe buckles. At his side he also wore a sword encased in polished white leather. In his left hand he held a cocked hat and yellow gloves.

As Christmas merrymakers filed into the room set aside for the festivities, a groom inquired each person's name, then the groom announced them. Washington gave a formal bow, without shaking hands, and gestured to his wife. Deliberately refraining from shaking hands, she also gave a graceful curtsy and pointed to the punch bowl. Chairs had been removed from the room so no thoughtless guest would sit in the presence of the president.

Guests sipped eggnog made from a secret recipe and nibbled dainty slices of a Christmas cake that Martha had baked for the occasion. Her recipe called for forty eggs, four pounds of butter, five pounds of fruit, and plenty of French brandy.

Once the last guests departed, the president and his wife exchanged gifts, which usually concluded their Christmas activities. One year there was an exception, however. Early in his second term, the normally solemn president had great fun drawing up a special employment contract for the rehiring of a gardener who had been

Abigail Adams

dismissed for drinking. Solemnly presented to Philip Bater on December 25, it forbade him to be "disguised with liquor" except at specified times, one of which promised him "four Dollars at Christmas with which he may be drunk four days and four nights."

John and Abigail Adams were the first to occupy the mansion known today as the White House. When they decided to give a children's party, they began a custom that is still in vogue. Suzanna, their four-year-old granddaughter, was guest of honor.

Following the custom of the Washingtons, the president and his lady stood formally in the Oval Room, which was lavishly decorated with greenery. The children were served punch and cake.

Suddenly a little girl dropped some of the splendid new dishes that the president had selected for his granddaughter's dollhouse, breaking at least one of them. Suzanna dashed across the room, surveyed the damage, then seized a doll from the arms of the offender, and bit off its nose. Thus she brought the first White House Christmas party for children to an abrupt end.

Thomas Jefferson served imported dainties and played the violin for his guests.

Thomas Jefferson, the third president, came to the Executive Mansion as a widower and urged his two daughters to bring their families to Washington for the holidays. He was delighted when they did so, and in 1805 he walked to the market to pick out a goose for dinner himself.

A noted lover of good food, Jefferson brought a French chef to the mansion and gave him a free hand with Christmas. As a result, children and adults were offered Dutch waffles, candied fruits, imported anchovies, and cheese, along with roast goose and other traditional holiday delicacies. During at least two Christmas parties, the president called for his violin and played favorite tunes for the guests.

There was no music for the James Madisons and their intimates at Christmas 1814. British troops, who had entered the capital on August 24, had seized and systematically looted the Executive Mansion. Following orders from Rear Adm. George Cockburn, 150 British sail-

During James Madison's tenure, the Executive Mansion was burned by British soldiers. Painted white to cover the smoke damage, it became the White House.

ors smashed windows and piled furniture in the middle of rooms. Then they put matches to oil-soaked rags and used poles to hurl balls of fire through the broken windows. Heavy rain prevented the complete destruction of the mansion, and a liberal application of white paint to cover the fire-darkened exterior walls was the source of the mansion's new name: the White House.

While waiting for their home to be repaired, the First Family lived for several weeks with Dolley Madison's sister, in full view of the badly damaged mansion. Later they moved into a house vacated by the French ambassador. Spending the 1814 holiday season in the home known as the Octagon, the Madisons found that its main rooms had only one door each, which caused visitors to mass in a narrow stair hall. For this reason Christmas parties were limited to a few close advisers and intimate friends.

Dolley Madison

A generation later, it was Andrew Jackson who used the Executive Mansion for the first elaborate Christmas party for children. Friends and foes alike usually called him Old Hickory, but during the holidays his action showed him to have a much softer heart than the nickname might suggest.

The 1835 party was given in honor of the two children of his adopted son and the four children of his niece and hostess, and the invitation read: "The children of President Jackson's family request you to join them on Christmas Day, at four o'clock P.M., in a frolic in the East Room."

Although they had no idea what to expect, about one hundred eager boys and girls attended. They found the East Room decorated for the first time with holly and mistletoe, and they enjoyed a great fight with "snowballs" made of cotton coated with starch. Frozen ices prepared by the president's chef were mostly shaped like fruit, but the centerpiece was an elaborate "frosted pine tree with animals standing at its base."

Andrew Jackson revealed that he had a soft heart, at least during the Christmas season.

After the small guests left, Jackson took his niece and hostess, Mary Emily Donelson, for a holiday ride. On their jaunt he delivered snuff to Mrs. James Madison and a hand-painted mirror to future president Martin Van Buren, who was famous for his vanity.

Van Buren came to the children's party the following year, performing for them as he never did for adults. Standing on one leg, the future president gobbled repeatedly and sang, "Here I stand all ragged and dirty; if you don't kiss me, I'll run like a turkey!" When order was restored, he and the president joined the children in playing blind man's buff, puss-in-the-corner, and hide-and-seek.

At his last Christmas in the White House, Andrew Jackson acted on impulse and invited children to his bedroom to hang their stockings. One youngster had an inspiration: Why not hang a stocking for the president so he could learn what Santa thought of *him*? Nodding consent, Old Hickory commented that he had waited nearly seventy years to put up a Christmas stocking. When he took it down the next day, he found in it a pair of warm slippers, a bag of tobacco, and a corncob pipe.

Believing that the Mexican War was about to end at Christmas 1847, James K. Polk authorized a radical change at the White House. Gas

The White House as it appeared during the presidency of James K. Polk.

lights were installed, replacing candles and lamps. There was no party for children, but adults were invited to a gala reception.

A newspaper reporter who attended did not describe the decorations or food, but he wrote:

> The First Lady of the Land was seated on a sofa, engaged with some half a dozen ladies in lively conversation. A shrewd and handsome woman, Mrs. Polk was better looking and better dressed than any of her female acquaintances. She wore a maroon-colored velvet dress with short sleeves, trimmed with very deep lace. Her handsome pink head-dress, brilliant under the glow of gas lights, caught the eyes of all observers.
>
> President Polk stood gracefully before the open fire, bowing and shaking hands as though he were an ordinary citizen. Brilliance of the illumination from the new gas lights was such that many, if not most, ladies shaded their eyes with their hands.

James K. Polk [BRADY STUDIO PHOTOGRAPH, NATIONAL ARCHIVES]

Mrs. Herbert Hoover made a firm rule: no reporters in the White House at Christmas.

Lou Hoover, wife of President Herbert Hoover, hated publicity and refused to have reporters in the White House during Christmas parties and other special holiday activities when her husband was president.

Reporter Bess Furman, who already had made a name for herself, was stopped at the door of the mansion when she appeared two days before Christmas. "Mrs. Hoover is busy making arrangements for Girl Scouts to come tomorrow," the doorman explained. "Come back some time next week," he suggested.

On impulse, Furman hurried to the Little House on New York Avenue, the local center of Girl Scout activity. Gertrude Bowman, who was in charge, listened with interest as Furman described what she called "discrimination against adults." With possible headline news for her organization in the balance, Bowman nodded assent when the reporter described a plan of operation.

That is how diminutive Bess Furman came to wear a Girl Scout uniform on Christmas Eve. Dawdling at a street corner near the White House, she spotted an approaching band of more than forty girls practicing some of the carols they expected to sing for the president and the First Lady.

"It was almost ridiculously easy to join the pack," she later recalled. "More than anything, I wanted to find out for myself just what takes place in the White House a few hours before Christmas Day. Once I saw that none of the Girl Scouts paid any attention to me, I knew I had it made.

"We went into the mansion and lined up in the front foyer, with the Marine Band waiting to play for us. Our first carol was 'The First Noel,' and just as we started it the door of the Blue Room opened to reveal President and Mrs. Hoover in evening clothes holding the hands of two of their grandchildren."

Earlier, the secretary of the interior, Ray L. Wilbur, had escorted the chief executive to a twilight ceremony in Sherman Square. By pressing a button, Hoover had lighted a spruce that in 1929 was called the community Christmas tree, the sixth to be set aglow by a president.

Beaming at the excited Girl Scouts, Hoover gestured for them to come into the East Room. "Wait a minute," interrupted his wife. "These girls sing so beautifully that I want to hear more. How about 'Good King Wenceslas'?"

According to the imposter's vivid first-hand account, the girls also sang "Joy to the World" and "Silent Night." Then they filed into the East Room, where each—Bess Furman included—was handed a candle taken from a tree whose tip touched the ceiling.

Eleanor Roosevelt, who was a determined fighter for women's rights before the term came into general use, demanded and got new privileges for women reporters. That meant it was no longer necessary for them to wear disguises to have access to the First Family during the holiday season.

Herself a newspaper columnist, Eleanor Roosevelt opened press conferences to women reporters.

Several male members of the White House press corps, along with a few women, watched on December 23, 1939, as President and Mrs. Roosevelt received 235 members of their staff in his office. After aides shook hands with them, presidential secretary Stephen Early handed each a Christmas gift. When opened, the packages were found to contain sterling silver key rings to which were attached miniature likenesses of the president's Scottie pup, Falla.

On Christmas Eve, Roosevelt delivered a message to the nation by radio following the 5:11 P.M. lighting of the National Christmas Tree. With Europe engulfed in war, the president told the nation that it could be a Merry Christmas "if we avoid defeatism and resolve to live more purely in the spirit of Christ."

Following a long-established family custom, Roosevelt gathered all members of the family together after dinner and read to them an abbreviated version of Dickens's *A Christmas Carol.* He ended by observing, "Because Bob Cratchit's humble home is a counterpart of millions of our own American homes, the story has stirring significance every year." Members of the family then hung their stockings on the president's mantelpiece.

On Christmas morning, Franklin Roosevelt III gleefully led his relatives to the president's bedroom. Beginning with the boy and ending with the president's wife Eleanor, they emptied their stockings, opened their packages, and exclaimed over their gifts. Even Falla had a stocking that contained a beautifully wrapped rubber bone.

At midmorning the extended family went in a body to inter-denominational church services at the First Congregational Church. Two hours later, five Basque boys and two girls appeared at the White House, dressed in native costume. They sang Basque carols, then gave Mrs. Roosevelt a manger scene made to resemble a Basque farm.

"It was our last truly joyful holiday season in the White House," Eleanor Roosevelt later told audiences. "My husband was dreadfully afraid—correctly, as events proved—that our nation would soon be engulfed in the horror of another war. But I vividly remember that in his radio message he urged all Americans to 'thank God for the interlude of Christmas!'"

Harry S Truman

One-time haberdasher Harry S Truman never had the exuberant Christmas sessions favored by Roosevelt. His only standard ceremony was the carving of the holiday turkey at the table while his daughter Margaret made photographs.

While he was president, members of the press did not know that Truman had called two aides aside in 1945 to launch a custom that prevailed during his tenure. The men were given responsibility for "finding two needy families, one black and one white," and seeing to it that "they have a really happy Christmas dinner" paid for by Harry Truman.

During Truman's presidency, the nation heard a peacetime Christmas Eve message from the White House for the first time since 1941. Standing in a spot where the snow had been cleared from the lawn, in the glow of the colored lights on the twenty-five-foot National Christmas Tree that had been unlighted for four years, the president invoked the spirit of the prophet Isaiah.

"With war ended, we must not fail or falter," he urged. "Peace has its victories no less hard won than success at arms. It is my Merry Christmas and Happy New Year wish to the world that it will make real the ancient promise, 'They shall beat their swords into plowshares and their spears into pruning-hooks; nation shall not lift up sword against nation, neither shall they learn war any more.'"

President Eisenhower was famous for his grin.

In 1956 Dwight D. Eisenhower welcomed Robert George of Anaheim, California, as a volunteer Santa Claus. Mamie Eisenhower was so delighted by his "Ho-ho-ho!" that she exclaimed, "You're the most beautiful Santa Claus I've ever seen!"

Standing within earshot, the president grinned and declared, "I'm appointing you the official White House Santa."

Annually thereafter for much of a decade, the California Santa made his trek to the capital, taking his sleigh along, to participate in the lighting of the National Christmas Tree.

John F. Kennedy once requested and received permission to drive the sleigh that came from California. He jokingly asked Santa to give it to him for Christmas, but it was not given to him.

Jacqueline Kennedy permanently altered White House tradition regarding entertaining children. For years, children of the family and those of diplomats and staff members had been invited to the Christmas parties. Mrs. Kennedy did not overlook them, but she added the names of many poor children of the nation's capital to the list.

In 1968, Lady Bird Johnson expanded upon Jacqueline Kennedy's idea. For a Metropolitan Opera Company presentation of *Hansel and Gretel*, she brought more than two hundred underprivileged children into the East Room.

Jacqueline Kennedy added underpriviledged children to Christmas guest lists.

President and Mrs. Gerald R. Ford received an unusual gift in 1976. Supporters in Michigan sent them an eighteen-foot Douglas fir that had been planted in 1949, the year Ford entered Congress. It was decorated with two thousand homemade ornaments from all over the United States and was topped by a corn husk angel.

However, the Fords did not see that tree on Christmas Day. For them, the season meant a skiing vacation. In Vail, Colorado, Betty Ford said that all she wanted for Christmas was "happiness, love, and having the family together."

Rosalyn Carter's most important change in the White House tree, made in 1977, was the hanging of 1,500 handmade ornaments that had been produced by retarded persons. For the first time, the White House was visited by a theater company for children, the Pixie Judy Troupe from the Copacabana Club in New York City. A gingerbread house, traditional in the Executive Mansion for so long that no one knows when it started, for the first time bore a name: Amy.

Deeply troubled by Iran's holding of hostages, Jimmy Carter ordered the strangest-ever lighting of a White House Christmas tree.

Two years later, the usual festive mood was absent. When it came time to light the National Christmas Tree, Jimmy Carter made a surprise announcement. It would remain dark except for a single star cluster at the top "until the hostages held in Iran come home."

Reminded of that promise as his last Christmas in the White House approached, Carter deviated from his pledge because of opposition from the National Park Service and the public. Thus in 1980 Americans learned of the strangest Christmas tree lighting in the history of the presidency.

Lights on the National Christmas Tree glowed for precisely 417 seconds, one second for each day the American hostages had been held captive in Iran. Then the thirty-foot Colorado spruce became black again, except for the stars of hope that twinkled brightly at the top.

"They Shall Be Offered Uniforms!"

"JOHN, TIME IS GETTING SHORT. HAVE YOU MADE all the necessary preparations?"

"I hope I have, Mr. President," assistant secretary John M. Hay responded. "This is the first time I have had to prepare for Senator Sumner on my own."

"But I hope you have assisted John Nicolay often enough to know what to do. He would have been here himself had I been informed earlier of the senator's desire for an urgent conference. I told Nicolay he could take Christmas Eve as a holiday."

"Of course, Mr. Lincoln. I understand completely, but you can see I am a bit nervous. I am to escort Senator Sumner up the grand staircase, which I do not use myself even once a month."

"It would not be fitting to bring a man of his dignity—and a cockleburr under my saddle, to boot—up the service stairs. Our city's most outspoken abolitionist would not realize that most of my intimates take this route, and he might take offense. I cannot afford to risk that."

"I understand, Mr. President. I have made your office tidy. There's not a scrap of paper on your desk."

"Good. And you have placed my cane in a storage closet?"

"I completely forgot, Mr. President. It is in its usual place. Once I have removed it from sight, I believe everything will be in order."

Abraham Lincoln with gold watch chain, but minus his prized walking cane [BRADY STUDIO PORTRAIT, NATIONAL ARCHIVES].

Seated behind his desk and waiting for the visitor whose presence he dreaded, Abraham Lincoln grimaced as he thought of the nearly forgotten cane. Months earlier, the president had instructed his chief secretary always to remove it when Charles Sumner of Massachusetts was expected. It might serve as a reminder that Congressman Preston

Brooks of South Carolina had used a gold-headed cane to club the senator into unconsciousness. That ugly incident on the floor of the U.S. Senate came as a result of Sumner's vitriolic attack upon slaveholders. Still hobbling from the brutal beating, Sumner could be expected to be even more tart than usual if he was reminded of the instrument wielded by Congressman Brooks.

"Delighted to see you, my dear sir," Lincoln exclaimed when the senator reached his office. "You must excuse the confusion here. Mrs. Lincoln is busy preparing to serve Christmas dinners to our brave men who lie wounded in the hospitals."

"I had to come," Sumner responded. "Time is running out. Here it is Wednesday night, and your Emancipation Proclamation—tardy as it is—is due to take effect a week from tomorrow. You know I am not a man to bite my tongue. I have come to ask you to order your military commanders to open their ranks and enlist those freed slaves who wish to join their units."

Abraham Lincoln struggled with the role of blacks in states loyal to the Union [1864 LITHOGRAPH, EHRGOTT, FORBIGER AND COMPANY; LIBRARY OF CONGRESS].

"That topic has been under urgent consideration for months, Senator," the president replied.

"Of course it has," snapped Sumner. "But nothing of consequence has been done. It appears to some of us that it will be an empty gesture to free the slaves in Rebel territory unless immediate steps are taken to make places for them in our fighting forces."

"Mr. Hay," Lincoln responded, gesturing to the assistant secretary, "please bring the summary of our actions concerning Negroes that John Nicolay prepared. Here, take this chair near the light so that you may read it and refresh Senator Sumner's memory, and mine as well."

"You want the entire document read?"

"Yes. Don't bother trying to make complete sentences. Just read the items as they are listed."

Visibly nervous, John Hay opened a packet of documents and began to read:

Senator Charles Sumner was an avid abolitionist and long-time critic of Abraham Lincoln.

> March 1862: Senator Sumner confronted Mr. Lincoln, demanding, "Do you know who is at this moment the largest slaveholder in the United States? It is you, sir, for you hold all the three thousand slaves of the District of Columbia, which is more than any other person in the country holds."
>
> April: Congress authorized government to buy D.C. slaves at not more than two hundred dollars a head and set them free. Border states strongly opposed to bill. Mr. Lincoln considered veto. Succeeded in getting new passage included, providing for free steamship tickets to Liberia or Haiti for any freed slave who would use them. Bill then signed.
>
> May: Senator Sumner quoted by many newspapers, "How slow this child called Freedom is being born!"

Leaning toward the president, Sumner flashed a rare smile. "You seem to have compiled a dossier of my words and deeds," he interjected.

"No, sir, just a few of the most memorable of them, Senator. Keep reading, John."

May: Congress passed act recognizing black republics. State Department followed by announcement that no Negro could be received as a foreign diplomat, not even if from Haiti or Liberia.

June: Minister from Haiti arrived. Received at Executive Mansion.

"I heard only rumors at the time. Why was this action on your part not given the publicity it deserved?" Sumner demanded.

Abraham Lincoln rose from his chair, clapped his hands together, and replied, "You do not read the *Springfield Republican.* If you did, you'd have found the editor quoting me as saying, 'You can tell the president of Haiti that I shan't tear my shirt if he decides to send a nigger here!'

"Of course, I never said anything of the sort. I simply tried to act the part of the president of the United States when the black ambassador arrived. I wish you could have been here, the evening he came to dinner, Senator. He said everybody in Haiti loves you. Mr. Hay, did your colleague happen to jot down the exact words of the ambassador as he left?"

"No, sir. Wait a minute. I think he did, sir. Yes. Here it is. He exclaimed, 'Signor Carlos il Senatore! Why his picture is in every cottage. He has done everything for us!' "

"Not quite everything," Sumner growled. "In fact, not nearly as much as I would have liked to do. I am amazed that you have kept such meticulous records and are able to put your hands on them. But I think I have heard enough to know that my name appears many times. There's no need to continue with this recital, Mr. Lincoln. Why don't we get to the business at hand?"

"Freed slaves as fighting men . . ." the President mused. "You may put your papers aside, Mr. Hay. My own memory is keen concerning a visit from Sen. James Harlan of Iowa and his supporters. "Senator Harlan urged me to free and to arm the slaves. That was some time late last spring. The exact date does not matter."

"Do you recall your response?" Sumner inquired.

"Certainly! I said, 'Gentlemen, I have put thousands of muskets into the hands of loyal citizens of Tennessee, Kentucky, and western

Members of the Fifty-fourth Massachusetts Colored Infantry charged Fort Wagner, South Carolina, on September 18, 1863 [HARPER'S WEEKLY].

North Carolina. They said they would defend themselves if they had guns. I have given them the guns. Now these men do not believe in mustering in the Negro. If I do it, these thousands of muskets will be turned against us. We should lose more than we should gain.'"

"Was that statement the source of rumors that you threatened to resign from office if forced to act against your conscience?"

"It was, Senator. And both of us know that Ben Wade of Ohio was quoted as saying, 'I hope to God you will, Mr. President.'"

"An unfortunate and a rash remark," Sumner growled. "Both of us also know that loyal Americans everywhere owe the preservation of the Union itself to your unswerving determination."

"Perhaps. But that is beside the point. When the Emancipation Proclamation goes into effect a few days from now, we shall find out how much value some Americans put upon the Union."

"Sentiment in loyal states is overwhelmingly in favor of this action, Mr. President. Did not sixteen governors meet with you a few days ago and pledge their unqualified support?"

"They did. But I cannot forget that a pamphlet by a former justice of the Supreme Court is being widely circulated. Benjamin R. Curtis is charging that in my office as president I have yielded to military necessity and am about to overturn established law and the Constitution."

"Two or three generations from now, many black Americans will look back with pride. They will rejoice that, given an opportunity to fight for freedom, their ancestors did so with a vengeance!"
— Abraham Lincoln

"Curtis represents a minority, and a small one at that," Sumner answered.

"Perhaps. I am not so sure. One of the reasons for what you yourself have often called my unreasonable delay stems from reactions in the border states. Without exception, leaders who are loyal to the Union have warned against hasty decisions of vexatious questions about slaves, and what to do with them once they are freed.

"Many of these persons—not all of them, by any means—have become reconciled to emancipation within states and regions now in rebellion. That clearly does *not* mean that they and their followers are ready to see us put freed slaves into uniform and hand them weapons."

"We may simply have to write off the border states," Senator Sumner responded sharply. "I am far more concerned about our own military leaders than about Andrew Johnson and his like."

"I am glad to hear you say that, Senator. I've been sitting here wondering when I ought to take the bit between my teeth and tell you what I have already done and am about to do.

"Knowing that publication of the preliminary Emancipation Proclamation was sure to stir up questions, I have consulted with some of our finest generals. Lorenzo Thomas has already volunteered to go to Mississippi, if necessary, to direct recruitment of Negro troops."

"Such an expedition may help us fill our ranks, but I am not convinced that it is essential," Sumner responded. "We have a considerable number of free blacks in my own state of Massachusetts. Some of them are indignant that the government will use them as laborers but will not permit them to fight."

Done at the city of Washington, this first day of
January, in the year of our Lord one thousand
eight hundred and sixty three, and of the
(L.S.) Independence of the United States
of America the eighty-seventh.

Abraham Lincoln

By the President;
William H. Seward,
Secretary of State

Eight days after having decided to use blacks as soldiers, Abraham Lincoln signed and issued the Emancipation Proclamation.

"Free blacks are not numerous enough to be important," the president insisted. "But God alone knows how many slaves there are in those states that have rebelled. If even a small fraction of the total number should escape to our lines, they could turn the tide in our struggle."

"How many, Mr. President?"

"God alone knows. Fifty thousand, at least. Maybe twice as many.

"I have kept you in suspense long enough, Senator. Before you arrived, I guessed your mission. But I wanted to give you a chance to speak and to hear from me.

"Only my most intimate advisers know of my decision. What I now tell you must be kept in strict confidence until official announcements are made a few days hence.

"I have considered all alternatives, I believe: gradual emancipation with compensation, colonization of freed slaves, and a re-united nation half slave, half free. In deciding to put into effect the Emancipation Proclamation drafted months ago and circulated in newspapers of the world, I carefully considered the question of military service.

"Not until this very week did I reach a decision. Few of our military commanders know it, but in this holiday season I have concluded that the best gift I can give to Negroes—and to our fighting forces—is the opportunity for freed slaves to serve in special units of the United States Army and the United States Navy."

"You really mean it, don't you, Mr. Lincoln?"

"I do. And I will ever remain grateful to you, Senator Sumner, for your part in helping me to arrive at this painful conclusion from which there can be no turning back. Two or three generations from now, many black Americans will look back with pride. They will rejoice that, given an opportunity to fight for freedom, their ancestors did so with a vengeance!"

As the long-time political antagonists shook hands and parted, neither the president accused of fence-straddling nor the fiery abolitionist senator realized that freedmen would soon rush to enlist. They formed the Fifty-fourth Massachusetts fighting unit, depicted in the motion picture *Glory,* widely hailed as perhaps the finest Civil War movie ever made.

Infinitely more important at the time than a far-in-the-future movie, was the fact that black soldiers donned blue uniforms at a much faster rate than either Abraham Lincoln or Charles Sumner envisioned. Before the end of the war waged to preserve the Union, Federal ranks included an estimated 180,000 blacks, at least 20,000 more than the total number of Confederate soldiers mustered on December 24, 1862.

"It Is Time to Bury the Past"

"NOW THAT THANKSGIVING IS OVER, IT WILL soon be Christmas."

"That won't mean a thing to me, Papa."

"Don't say such things as that, Eliza. Just the other day at the War Department, I heard a doctor tell about a man who got over his slow consumption."

"That was a man, Papa, and I'm a woman. Besides, the proper name is phthisis."

"I know that, but I can't ever pronounce it right. Just let me stick with 'slow consumption.' Maybe Christmas will give your health a boost."

"I'm about as well as I ever expect to be. But why are you talking about my health at the holiday season? You must have something up your sleeve."

"Well, maybe," the former military governor of Tennessee responded. And so President Andrew Johnson began to talk with his wife about an idea.

"I'm thinking maybe I ought to extend my amnesty proclamation. And not leave anybody out this time."

"Why, Andrew Johnson. If you are not mighty careful, you will have Charles Sumner and the rest of the Radical Republicans after you with an ax. If I understand things properly, you didn't leave out many Rebels in 1865."

"Maybe. But back then I was concentrating on the states. I was trying to make it easier for them to get back into the Union, and all I really did was to add a little to President Lincoln's plan."

"You added a whole lot," Eliza Johnson answered as she propped herself up in bed and pointed a finger at her husband, "and I'm proud

Eliza Johnson, an invalid, doubted the wisdom of a presidential pardon for Jefferson Davis.

of you for doing it! But those wolves over on Capitol Hill never say anything about how you made it *harder* for some folks in Tennessee."

"Mother, not a thing I did was aimed at Tennessee. You were with me there, and it seemed personal when it wasn't. Everybody in Rebel territory was treated alike, and some of those fellows profited from the war, in spite of all the complaining they have done."

"How many who fought for the Confederacy have swallowed their pride and taken the oath of allegiance since 1865?" Eliza asked.

"Thousands and thousands. I doubt if anybody knows exactly how many. But that didn't keep a lot of fine Southerners from wading across the Rio Grande into Mexico. Or taking a fast ship to Brazil," the president answered.

Then he continued, "I know some of them would come back if they could. We've bled ourselves enough by now. On both sides. I think it is about time to see if we can't bury the past. You know what I think of Jefferson Davis. But he's a human being and an American, and Christmas is the time to turn him loose."

Sinking back upon her pillow and fanning herself vigorously, Johnson's wife blurted, "You've always despised him! How in the world can you be thinking of doing something nice for him now?"

Shaking his head in bewilderment, the chief executive brought his wife up to date on developments in the case. Captured in Georgia while trying to flee the country, Jefferson Davis was immediately charged with treason. Court after court tried to deal with the matter, but none seemed able to decide what should be done with the ex-president of the Confederate States of America. More than one justice declared that Davis should hang, but then turned around and quoted Abraham Lincoln's famous statement in which he dared to hope that when war ended there would be "no bloody work of hanging for treason."

"Now there's a motion to quash the indictment against Davis," Johnson explained. "It is likely to come to trial in the next thirty days."

"Who will decide the case?"

"Chief Justice Chase will have a lot to say about the matter. Everybody thinks he favors quashing the indictment so as to heal old wounds. But Underwood, the district judge who will hear the case with him, is dead set against any leniency."

"Andrew, this is a matter for the judges to settle. I don't see what you can do. You are not a judge."

"No, Mother, I am not a judge. But until my term expires, I am president of the United States. Some nights I can't sleep for thinking about what Sherman said."

Andrew Johnson then pulled a slip of paper from his pocket and unfolded it, although he had memorized every word: "'I am sick and tired of war. Its glory is all moonshine. It is only those who have never fired a shot nor heard the shrieks and groans of the wounded who cry aloud for blood, more vengeance, more desolation.'

"We have to quit looking for more vengeance if this country is ever going to get over the war," the president continued. "And it seems to me that the day on which Jesus Christ was born is just the right time to put a stop to the cry for blood. Far too many powerful men think it will make us a better nation to put a noose around the neck of a man who was perhaps the finest secretary of war we have ever had.

Charged with treason, Jefferson Davis was the first recipient of a Christmas pardon.

"I've had my aides studying the Constitution, and I've even re-read it two or three times myself. There are some things that the president can manage and that no one else on the top side of the earth can do. Right now, Congress is chewing on a bill aimed at limiting the power of the president. If I don't act soon, I may not be able to act at all."

Bending over his wife, Johnson apologized for bothering her with his worries, then retired to his office. "Try to get some sleep," he said. "I'll do a lot of thinking and maybe a little praying before I make up my mind what to do, if anything."

In early December, Judges Chase and Underwood heard a motion to quash Jefferson Davis's indictment for treason. They rendered a split decision, and the case was certified to the U.S. Supreme Court for a final decision.

On December 25 the president put his political future on the line by signing a document that granted "general amnesty" to former Confederates. Jefferson Davis was no longer on trial for his life, and all war participants, except high-ranking civil and military officials, were granted an unconditional pardon. Fugitives who had fled from the United States could return home.

The proclamation also relieved the former president of the Confederacy from further prosecution. After his case was nol-prossed in Richmond a few weeks later, Davis was discharged.

As Eliza Johnson had predicted, many of her husband's enemies on Capitol Hill were furious at his Christmas amnesty. Although it was received with rejoicing throughout the South and in time did much to heal sectional wounds, it aroused bitter anger among members of Congress.

Andrew Johnson's precedent made the White House the site of other notable pardons during the Christmas season.

Pardoned socialist Eugene Debs was met by photographers when he stepped from Atlanta's Federal Penitentiary.

Socialist Eugene Debs, sentenced to ten years in prison for opposition to World War I, was pardoned on December 24, 1921. Simultaneously, President Warren G. Harding freed twenty-three other political prisoners.

On December 23, 1933, Franklin D. Roosevelt proclaimed a Christmas amnesty for 1,500 persons who had violated the Espionage Act during World War I. Most of them had served time in prison and had been stripped of voting rights and other civil liberties. These rights were restored to them by Roosevelt's proclamation.

President Harry S. Truman chose Christmas Eve 1945 as the day on which to pardon ex-convicts who had volunteered for military

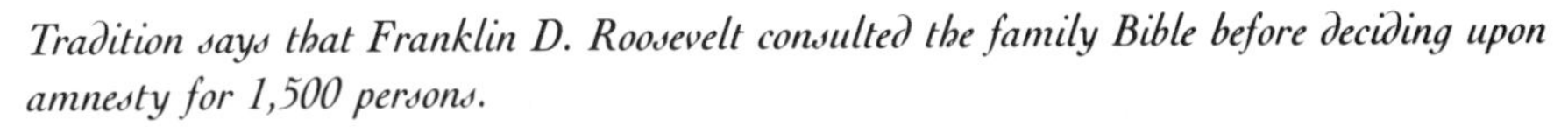

Tradition says that Franklin D. Roosevelt consulted the family Bible before deciding upon amnesty for 1,500 persons.

service. Vigorously opposed by many lawmakers, his action restored full civil and political rights to a large group of Americans.

Exactly two years later, Truman acted again. This time his Christmas Eve pardon affected 1,523 draft evaders then in prison or recently released but still deprived of civil rights. On Christmas Eve 1952, Truman pardoned still another large group of former prisoners who had served in the peacetime army, as well as hundreds of peacetime deserters from the military.

Like Jefferson Davis, Harry Truman devoted his retirement years to writing.

No one knows how many thousands of Americans have been affected by presidential pardons issued at Christmas. Most of them were low-level offenders whose names have long since been forgotten.

Jefferson Davis, first and by far the most prominent beneficiary of holiday leniency by the Oval Office, retired to his Mississippi estate soon after being pardoned. There he spent more than three years writing a two-volume account of *The Rise and Fall of the Confederate Government.*

Andrew Johnson, who launched the custom of issuing pardons at Christmas, infuriated his political foes by this exercise of "extraordinary power." Brought before the bar of the U.S. Senate by a bill of impeachment, the only chief executive who has faced that ordeal was cleared of charges by a single vote. In private, he often fumed that he would have enjoyed seeing Davis hang, but the climate of the times persuaded him that, for the good of the nation, he should "behave like a good Christian on the day of Christ's birth."

Peace in a World of Storm

ABSOLUTE SECRECY UNTIL I ARRIVE. NO ONE, REPEAT, NO ONE, MUST KNOW THAT I AM ON THE WAY.

CHURCHILL

"OBVIOUSLY, IT IS IMPOSSIBLE TO ABIDE BY the letter of this request. Those of you who work in the code room have already had access to the news. Some of our key officials will have to be informed, also."

"What about guards?"

"They do not need to know. We will simply order more units and inform them that absolute secrecy is a must."

"Will you tell Mrs. Roosevelt?"

"I believe that would violate the spirit of Mr. Churchill's request."

Then President Franklin D. Roosevelt smiled broadly and added, "Of course, I cannot guarantee that she will not discover what is going on. Certain household arrangements will have to be made, and all of you know that my wife has a great nose for news!"

A "boy idealist"—young Winston Churchill.

Having traveled from London by air, the prime minister of Great Britain reached Washington, D.C., in secrecy. Even the motorcade that took him to the White House went unnoticed in the turmoil of the times. During the two weeks since the bombing of Pearl Harbor, life had taken on a new quality for those living and working in the nation's capital.

President Franklin D. Roosevelt was a past master of radio talks and "fireside chats."

Once inside the heavily guarded Executive Mansion and no longer in danger of assassination en route, Winston Churchill quickly relaxed. However, early on his first day as President Roosevelt's guest, he was faced with a decision.

"News of your arrival has leaked out," his host informed him, "and there has been an immediate request for a press conference. Are you up to it?"

"The notion of an American press conference is enough to make a brave man tremble!" Churchill chuckled, "but I will do my best. I have the greatest esteem for the press."

"Is part of that esteem based on your own experiences?" Roosevelt asked.

"Perhaps. You probably don't know it, but I was just twenty-one when I went to Cuba to cover the fighting there for the *Daily Graphic.*"

"No, Mr. Prime Minister, I was not aware of that early venture into print. But if my memory serves me correctly, you were a war correspondent for the *Morning Post* during the Boer War in Africa."

"Correct, Mr. President. And two years earlier, in India, I worked for the *Daily Telegraph.*"

Smiling broadly, the prime minister remembered, "The *Telegraph* paid me five pounds per column, big money in 1897!"

"Then I'll see to it that you are introduced to our corps of White House correspondents as a fellow member of the press!"

At the December 23 press conference, Churchill gave instant responses to most questions. Near its end, however, a reporter demanded, "Mr. Prime Minister, how long will it take to lick the Axis powers?"

Pondering for what seemed an eternity to some, the man charged with the military defense of Great Britain replied, "If we manage it well, it will take only half as long as if we manage it badly."

Congratulated by Roosevelt upon his response, Churchill thanked his host but insisted that he had not found it difficult. "At Harrow, where they called me 'Carrot Top,' I was put in the lowest division of the lowest class. I stayed at the bottom for a very long time—long

Roosevelt and Churchill conferred daily during the famous Casablanca Conference [LIBRARY OF CONGRESS].

enough to give me a great advantage over the clever students. They proceeded to master Latin and Greek and other splendid things.

"Meanwhile, I was taught the use of the English language, only, by Mr. Somervell. His responsibility was simple. He had to teach the slowest and most stupid boys at Harrow how to write mere English.

"As I remained at the bottom of the class three times as long as anyone else, I had three times as much of Mr. Somervell, a delightful man to whom I remain greatly indebted."

Chuckling, Franklin D. Roosevelt leaned far over in his wheelchair and demanded, "I take it, then, that you will not object if I schedule you for a Christmas Eve radio address to the American people?"

"I will be delighted! But I must warn you in advance that I cannot deliver one of your famous 'fireside chats.'"

"Done!" exclaimed the president. "We'll try to give you a live audience as well. We often have five thousand here for the lighting of the National Christmas Tree."

Although the weather was cold, an estimated twenty thousand people crowded against the black iron fence that surrounded the White House as they waited for the lighting of the tree. Those who were permitted inside the gate were warned, "No packages tonight, and no cameras."

President and Mrs. Roosevelt made their way to a balcony, followed by refugees from Norway who were their house guests, Crown Prince Olaf and Crown Princess Marthe. Flanked by cabinet members on each side, Churchill watched as a towering evergreen on the White House lawn sprang into light when Roosevelt pressed a button.

After an invocation by the rector of Catholic University, Roosevelt spoke briefly to the nation: "It is in the spirit of peace and good will, and with particular thoughtfulness of those, our sons and brothers, who serve in our armed forces on land and sea, near and far—those who serve and endure for us—that we light our Christmas candles

Prime Minister Winston Churchill with President Harry Truman, Roosevelt's successor.

now across this continent from one coast to the other on this Christmas evening.

"Now you will have an opportunity to hear from a visitor who wishes to share a few words with you at this most solemn of times: Mr. Winston Churchill, prime minister of Great Britain."

Churchill, who had been busy with other things and had managed to find barely twenty minutes in which to prepare his talk, stepped to the microphone and delivered one of the most memorable Christmas messages ever.

This is a strange Christmas Eve.

Almost the whole world is locked in deadly struggle, and with the most terrible weapons which science can devise, the nations advance upon each other.

Ill would it be for us this Christmastide if we were not sure that no greed for the land or wealth of other people, no vulgar ambition, no morbid lust for material gain at the expense of others, has led us to the field. Here, in the midst of war, raging and roaring over every land and every sea, creeping nearer to our own hearts and homes, here, amid all the tumult, we have tonight the peace of the spirit in each cottage home and in each generous heart.

Therefore, we may cast aside for this night at least the cares and dangers which beset us, and make for our children an evening of happiness in a world of storm. Here, then, for one night only, each home throughout the English-speaking world should be a brightly lighted island of happiness and peace.

Let all the children have their night of fun and laughter.

Let the gifts of Father Christmas delight their play.

Let us grown-ups share to the full in their unstinted pleasure before we turn again to the stern task and the formidable years that lie before us, resolved that by our sacrifice and daring, these same children shall not be robbed of their inheritance or denied their right to live in a free and decent world.

In God's mercy, a happy Christmas to you all.

How to Put This Volume to Double Use

A REMARKABLE PHENOMENON OF OUR TIMES HAS been the sudden emergence of storytelling as a form of art, instruction, and entertainment. Closely related to this development is the change in attitude toward authors. Instead of asking an author to make a talk or give a lecture these days, a program chairman is likely to urge, "Please give us some readings from your books."

The dynamic of this approach was realized at first hand a few years ago. Visiting in Savannah, Georgia, my wife and I noticed a placard inviting members of the public to a session at the Savannah College of Art and Design. Distinguished author James Dickey would read from his poems and novels, the announcement promised.

Perhaps you have been emotionally stunned by the stark brutality of episodes in the novel *Deliverance* or have become acquainted with some of Dickey's stirring poems. If so, you will not be surprised when I report that listening to readings by this literary giant turned out to be a powerful and unforgettable experience, comparable to hearing "Dream the Impossible Dream" sung on a Chicago stage or experiencing a great conductor and orchestra's subtle interpretation of Beethoven's *Fifth Symphony.*

Although the chance that you are a James Dickey is small, *you can do immeasurably better than you may think,* especially when inspired by the Christmas season.

This collection has been deliberately tailored for oral adaptation—storytelling, if you will—at civic, fraternal, social, and religious gatherings during the season it celebrates.

If you are called upon to make a suggestion about a program or to take a part in one, please say Yes! with enthusiasm. Then select one or more of the tales in this volume. Read it aloud two or three times, underline freely and make marginal notes, then make modifications appropriate for your personality and the planned occasion. When you have done this, the material will become yours in a very personal sense.

A single test will convince you that although storytelling is an art form, it is one that you can master. Once you have tried it, hopefully, you will be so delighted that you will be able to put *A Treasury of Christmas Stories* to effective use year after year, not simply as a book to be read but as a collection of stories to be shared with groups ranging from small children to their grandparents.

Index